SOLDIERS OF SALAMIS

SOLDIERS OF SALAMIS

Javier Cercas

Translated from the Spanish by Anne McLean

BLOOMSBURY

For Raül Cercas and Mercè Mas

This edition has been translated with the help of an aid from the Directorate General for Books, Archives and Libraries of the Ministry of Education, Culture and Sport, Spain

Published by Bloomsbury, New York and London
Distributed to the trade by Holtzbrinck Publishers

All papers used by Bloomsbury are natural, recyclable products made from wood grown in well-managed forests. The manufacturing processes conform to the environmental regulations of the country of origin.

Library of Congress Cataloging-in-Publication Data

Cercas, Javier, 1962-
[Soldados de Salamina. English]
Soldiers of Salamis / Javier Cercas ; translated from the Spanish by Anne McLean
p. cm.
ISBN 1-58234-384-5
1. Sánchez-Mazas, Rafael, 1894-1966–Fiction. 2. Spain–History–Civil War, 1936-1939–Fiction. I. McLean, Anne, 1962- II. Title.

PQ6653.E62S6613 2004
863'.64–dc22
2003062759

Originally Published in Spain as *Soldados de Salamina*
by Tusquets Editores, Barcelona, 2001
First U.S. Edition 2004

1 3 5 7 9 10 8 6 4 2

Typeset by Hewer Text Ltd, Edinburgh
Printed in the United States of America by
R.R. Donnelley & Sons, Crawfordsville

The gods desire to keep the stuff of life
Hidden from us.

Hesiod, *Works and Days*

AUTHOR'S NOTE

This book is the fruit of extensive reading and long conversations. Many of the people to whom I am indebted appear in the text with their full names; among those who do not, I want to mention Josep Clara, Jordi Gracia, Eliane and Jean-Marie Lavaud, José-Carlos Mainer, Josep Maria Nadal, Carlos Trías, and especially Mónica Carbajosa, whose doctoral thesis, *The Prose of '27: Rafael Sánchez Mazas*, has been immensely useful. To all of them: thank you.

CONTENTS

Translator's Foreword

Twentieth-century Spanish political history is extremely complex and the following is an attempt to give readers a brief outline of some of the background to parts of this novel.

Spain was declared a Republic, for the second time, on 14 April 1931 when King Alfonso XIII abdicated after monarchist parties were defeated in key municipal elections. The country was extremely polarized with vast numbers belonging to ideologically committed trade unions and parties across the political spectrum. National elections were held in November 1933, resulting in a right-wing government which collapsed a little over two years later. The elections of February 1936 were contested by two broad coalitions: the *Frente Nacional* and the *Frente Popular*.

The *Nacionales*, or Nationalists, were supported by the conservative, fascist, Catholic and monarchist parties. Among these was the *Falange Española* or Spanish Falange, a small fascist-style party, founded in 1933, which merged the following year with the JONS (*Juntas de Ofensiva Nacional-Sindicalista* / Juntas of the National-Syndicalist Offensive), a more proletarian fascist movement, in existence since 1931.

The Popular Front, an alliance of liberal and left-wing parties, won the elections by a slim margin and formed a government. The coalition included parties ranging from liberal and social democratic Republicans, through advocates of Basque or Catalan autonomy, to socialists, Trotskyists and Soviet-allied Communists. The Popular Front was also actively supported by the socialist General Workers' Union (UGT, *Unión General de Trabajadores*).

Spanish anarchism was a large-scale trade-union-based movement that fought for worker control of industry and agriculture. The National Confederation of Workers (CNT, *Confederación Nacional de Trabajo*) was particularly strong in Andalucia, Aragón and Catalonia. Opposed to so-called representative politics, they supported none of the parties of the Popular Front but were among the first to organize militias to defend the Republic.

The Civil War broke out on 18 July 1936 when a group of military officers, supported by elements from the Nationalist parties, attempted a coup d'état to overthrow the Popular Front government. They overcame resistance in the south and the west but in the two largest cities – Madrid and Barcelona – the rebellion was defeated by hastily organized militias and loyal members of the armed forces.

Despite the supply of arms and men to Franco's Nationalists by Mussolini and Hitler, Britain and France agreed a policy of non-intervention. The Republican government sent the Spanish gold reserves to Moscow to purchase badly needed weapons and thus provided the Communists with an influence disproportionate to their numbers, leading to bitter and deadly hostilities within the anti-fascist forces.

By early 1937 the Nationalists controlled the entire border with Portugal and much of northern Spain and the Basque country. In 1938 they cut the Republican zone in two and in July the Popular Army launched a huge offensive across the Ebro River. This extremely bloody battle initially caught the Nationalists off guard but in the end left the Republican forces exhausted and in January 1939, Barcelona fell to Franco's army. Half a million refugees crossed into France before the Nationalists sealed the border on 10 February. When Madrid fell on 27 March, tens of thousands more Republican soldiers and civilians fled to the Mediterranean coast at Alicante only to watch approaching rescue ships turn away in fear of being swamped. The last of the Republican front lines disintegrated towards the end of the month. Franco would accept only an unconditional surrender and declared the Civil War over on 1 April 1939.

A.M.

Part One

FOREST FRIENDS

IT WAS THE SUMMER of 1994, more than six years ago now, when I first heard about Rafael Sánchez Mazas facing the firing squad. Three things had just happened: first my father had died; then my wife had left me; finally, I'd given up my literary career. I'm lying. The truth is, of those three things, the first two are factual, even exact; but not the third. In reality, my career as a writer had never actually got started, so it would have been difficult to give it up. It'd be more accurate to say I gave it up having barely begun. I'd published my first novel in 1989; like the collection of stories that appeared two years earlier, the book was received with glaring indifference, but a combination of vanity and an enthusiastic review written by a friend from those days contrived to convince me I could one day become a novelist and, to do so, should quit my job as a journalist and devote myself entirely to writing. The results of this change in lifestyle were five years of economic, physical and metaphysical anguish, three unfinished novels and a dreadful depression that knocked me back into an armchair in front of the television for two whole months. Fed up with paying the bills, including the one for my father's funeral, and watching me stare at the blank television screen and weep, my wife moved out as soon as I started to recover, and I was left with no choice but to forget my literary ambitions and ask for my old job back at the newspaper.

I'd just turned forty, but luckily – or because I'm not a good writer but nor am I a bad journalist, or, more likely, because there was no one at the paper willing to do my job for a salary as meagre as mine – they agreed. They assigned me to the culture section, which is where they put people they don't know what to do with. At first, with the undeclared aim of punishing my disloyalty – given that, for some journalists, a colleague who leaves journalism to write a novel is nothing less than a traitor – they made me do everything but get the boss's coffee from the bar on the corner, and very few colleagues refrained from indulging in sarcasm and irony at my expense. Time must have blunted the memory of my infidelity: soon I was editing the odd piece, writing articles, doing interviews. That was how, in July 1994, I ended up interviewing Rafael Sánchez Ferlosio, who was giving a series of lectures at the university at the time. I knew Ferlosio was extremely reluctant to speak to journalists, but thanks to a friend (or rather a friend of that friend who'd organized Ferlosio's stay in the city), I managed to get him to agree to talk to me for a while. Calling that an interview would be going a bit far; if it was an interview, it was the weirdest one I've ever done. To begin with, Ferlosio showed up on the terrace of the Bistrot surrounded by a swarm of friends, disciples, admirers and hangers-on; this, added to an obvious lack of attention to his clothes and a physical appearance that inextricably blended the manner of a Castilian aristocrat ashamed of being one with that of an old Mongol warrior – massive head, unruly hair streaked with grey, hard, emaciated, difficult face, large nose and cheeks shadowed with incipient beard – might have suggested, to an uninformed observer, a religious guru surrounded by acolytes. Moreover, Ferlosio roundly refused to answer a single one of the questions I put to him, claiming he'd given the best answers he was capable of in his books. This doesn't mean he didn't want to talk to me; quite the contrary: as if seeking to refute his reputation for unsociability (or perhaps it's just unfounded), he was extremely cordial, and the afternoon flew by as we chatted. The problem was that if I asked him, say, about his division of literary personae into those of fate and those of character, he would contrive to answer me with a discourse on, say, the causes of the rout of the Persian fleet in the battle of Salamis; whereas when I tried to extract his opinion on, say, the pomp and ceremony of the celebrations of the five hundredth anniversary of the conquest of the Americas, he would answer me by describing, with a wealth of gesticulation and detail, say, the correct use of a jack plane. It was an exhausting tug-of-war, and it wasn't until the last beer of the evening that Ferlosio told the story of his father facing the firing squad, the story that's kept me in suspense for the last two years. I don't remember who mentioned the name Rafael Sánchez Mazas or how it came up (maybe it was one of Ferlosio's friends, maybe Ferlosio himself), but I do remember Ferlosio telling us:

'They shot him not far from here, at the Collell Sanctuary.' He looked at me. 'Have you ever been there? Me neither, but I know it's near Banyoles. It was at the end of the war. The 18th of July had caught him in Madrid, and he had to seek refuge in the Chilean Embassy, where he spent more than a year. Towards the end of '37 he escaped from the Embassy and left Madrid hidden in a truck, perhaps with the aim of getting to France. However, they arrested him in Barcelona and, when Franco's troops were about to reach the city, took him to Collell, up near the border. That's where they shot him. It was an execution by firing squad *en masse*, probably chaotic, because the war was already lost and the Republicans were rushing helter-skelter for the Pyrenees, so I don't think they knew they were executing one of the founders of the Falange, and a personal friend of José Antonio Primo de Rivera at that. My father always kept the trousers and sheepskin jacket he was wearing when they shot him, he showed them to me many times, they're probably still around; the trousers had holes in them, because the bullets only grazed him and he took advantage of the confusion of the moment to run and hide in the woods. From there, sheltering in a ditch, he heard the dogs barking and the shots and the soldiers' voices as they searched for him knowing they couldn't waste much time searching because Franco's troops were on their heels. At some point my father heard branches moving behind him; he turned and saw a militiaman looking at him. Then he heard a shout: "Is he there?" My father told how the soldier stared at him for a few seconds and then, without taking his eyes off him shouted, "There's nobody over here!", turned and walked away.'

Ferlosio paused, and his eyes contracted into a knowing expression of boundless mischief, like a little boy holding back his laughter.

'He spent several days hiding in the woods, living on what he could find or what they gave him at the farms. He didn't know the area, and moreover he'd broken his glasses, so he could hardly see; that's why he always said he'd never have survived if he hadn't met some lads from a nearby village – Cornellà de Terri it was called, or is – some lads who protected and fed him until the Nationalists arrived. They became great friends, and when it was all over he stayed at their house for a few days. I don't think he ever saw them again, but he talked to me about them more than once. I remember he always called them by the name they'd given themselves: "the forest friends".'

That was the first time I heard the story told, and that's how I heard it. As for the interview with Ferlosio, I finally managed to salvage it, or perhaps I made it up: as far as I recall, not once did he allude to the battle of Salamis (but he did discuss the distinction between personae of character and personae of fate), nor to the exact use of a jack plane (but did expound on the pomp of the five hundredth anniversary celebrations of the discovery of America). Nor did the interview mention the firing squad at Collell or Sánchez Mazas. Of the first I knew only what I'd just heard Ferlosio tell, of the latter not much more; at that time I'd not read a single line of Sánchez Mazas, and to me he was no more than a mist-shrouded name, just one more of the many Falangist politicians and writers that the last years of Spanish history had hastily buried, as if the gravediggers feared they weren't entirely dead.

As a matter of fact, they weren't. At least not entirely. The story of the writer facing the firing squad at Collell and the circumstances surrounding it had so intrigued me, that after interviewing Ferlosio I started to feel curious about Sánchez

Mazas; also about the Civil War, of which till then I'd known not much more than I did about the battle of Salamis or the exact use of the jack plane, and about the horrific stories that war produced, which till then I'd considered excuses for old men's nostalgia and fuel for the imagination of unimaginative novelists. Coincidentally (or maybe not so coincidentally), it became fashionable around that time for Spanish writers to rehabilitate Falangist writers. It had actually started earlier, in the mid-1980s, when certain refined, influential publishers released the occasional volume by some refined, forgotten Falangist, but by the time I became interested in Sánchez Mazas, in some literary circles they weren't just rehabilitating the good Falangist writers, but also the average and even the bad ones. Some ingenuous souls, including a few guardians of left-wing orthodoxy and the odd mischief-maker, declared that rehabilitating a Falangist writer was vindicating (or laying the groundwork to vindicate) Falangism itself. The truth was exactly the opposite: rehabilitating a Falangist writer was just rehabilitating a writer; or more precisely, it was vindicating themselves as writers by rehabilitating a good writer. I mean that the fashion arose, in the best cases (the worst aren't worth mentioning), from the natural need all writers have to invent their own tradition, from a certain urge to be provocative, from the problematic certainty that literature is one thing and life another and that it was therefore possible to be a good writer at the same time as being a terrible person (or a person who supports and foments terrible causes), from the conviction that we were being literarily unfair to certain Falangist writers, who, to use Andrés Trapiello's phrase, had won the war but lost literature. Be that as it may, Sánchez Mazas did not escape this collective disinterring: in 1986 his collected poetry was published for the first time; in 1995 a popular series included a new edition of his novel *The New Life of Pedrito de Andía*; in 1996 another of his novels, *Rosa Krüger*, also appeared in a new edition, having actually been out of print since 1984. I read all those books then. I read them with interest – with pleasure even – but not enthusiasm: it didn't take me long to conclude that Sánchez Mazas was a good writer, but not a great writer, though I doubt I'd have known how to clearly explain the difference between a great and a good writer. I remember, in the months or years that followed, randomly gathering bits and pieces about Sánchez Mazas from things I read, and even coming across the odd summary and vague allusion to the episode at Collell.

Time passed. I began to forget the story. One day at the beginning of February 1999, the year of the sixtieth anniversary of the end of the Civil War, someone at the paper suggested the idea of writing a commemorative article about the tragic last days of the poet Antonio Machado who, in January 1939 (together with his mother, his brother José and some hundreds of thousands of their utterly terrified compatriots), driven by the advance of Franco's troops, fled from Barcelona to Collioure, on the other side of the French border, where he died a short time later. The episode was very well known, and I rightly thought that not a single Catalan (or non-Catalan) journalist would manage to avoid recalling it at some point during the anniversary, so I'd resigned myself to writing the standard time-honoured article when I remembered Sánchez Mazas and that his botched execution had occurred more or less at the same time as Machado's death, except on the Spanish side of the border. I then imagined that the symmetry and contrast between these two terrible events – a kind of chiasmus of history – was perhaps not coincidental and that, if I could manage to get across the substance of each within the same article, the strange parallel might perhaps endow them with a new meaning. This belief took hold when, as I began to do a little research, I stumbled across the story of Manuel Machado's journey to Collioure, which he made shortly after the death of his brother Antonio. Then I started to write. The result was an article called 'An Essential Secret'. Since, in its way, it's also essential to this story, I include it here:

Sixty years have passed since the death of Antonio Machado in the last days of the Civil War. Of all the stories contained in that history, one of the saddest is no doubt Machado's, because it ends badly. It has been told many times. He came to Barcelona from Valencia in April 1938, accompanied by his mother and his brother José, and stayed first in the Hotel Majestic and later in the Torre de Castañer, an old mansion on Sant Gervasi avenue. There he kept doing what he'd been doing since the beginning of the war: using his writing to defend the legitimate government of the Republic. He was old, weary and ill, and he no longer believed in Franco's defeat. He wrote 'This is the end; any day now Barcelona will fall. For the strategists, for the politicians, for the historians, it is all clear: we have lost the war. But in human terms, I am not so sure. Perhaps we have won.' Who knows if he guessed right about that last bit; without doubt he was right about the first. The night of 22 January 1939, four days before Franco's troops took Barcelona, Machado and his family left in a convoy for the French border. Other writers accompanied them on that nightmarish exodus, among them Corpus Barga and Carles Riba. They made stops in Cervià de Ter and Mas Faixat, near Figueres. Finally, the night of the 27th, after walking 600 metres through the rain, they crossed the border. They'd been obliged to leave their luggage behind and they had no money. Thanks to the help of Corpus Barga, they managed to make it to Collioure and get rooms in the Hotel Bougnol Quintana. Less than a month later the poet died; his mother survived him by three days. In the pocket of his overcoat, his brother José found a few notes; one of them was a verse, perhaps the first line of his last poem: 'These blue days, this childhood sun.'

The story doesn't end here. Shortly after the death of his brother Antonio, the poet Manuel Machado, who lived in Burgos, learned of it through the foreign press. Manuel and Antonio were not just brothers, they were intimates. The uprising of 18 July had caught Manuel in Burgos, rebel territory; Antonio, in Madrid, Republican territory. It is reasonable to assume that, had he been in Madrid, Manuel would have been loyal to the Republic; it would perhaps be idle to speculate what might have happened if Antonio had chanced to be in Burgos. The fact is, as soon as he heard the news of his brother's death, Manuel procured a safe-conduct and, after travelling for days across a Spain that had been reduced to ashes, arrived in Collioure. At the hotel he learned his mother had also died. He went to the cemetery. There, before the graves of his mother and his brother Antonio, he met his brother José. They talked. Two days later Manuel returned to Burgos.

11

But the story — at least the story I now want to tell — doesn't end here either. At more or less the same time that Machado died in Collioure, Rafael Sánchez Mazas faced a firing squad near the Sanctuary of Collell. Sánchez Mazas was a good writer; he was also a friend of José Antonio, and one of the founders and ideologues of the Falange. His adventures in the war are shrouded in mystery. A few years ago his son, Rafael Sánchez Ferlosio, told me his version. I don't know whether or not it is strictly true; I'm just telling it as he told me. Trapped in Republican Madrid by the military uprising, Sánchez Mazas sought refuge in the Chilean Embassy. He spent most of the war there; towards the end he tried to escape hidden in the back of a truck, but they arrested him in Barcelona and, as Franco's troops approached the city, he was taken towards the border. Before crossing it they assembled a firing squad; but the bullets only grazed him, and he took advantage of the confusion to run and hide in the woods. From there he heard the voices of the militiamen pursuing him. One of them finally found him. He looked Sánchez Mazas in the eye. Then he shouted to his comrades 'There's nobody over here!', turned and walked away.

'Of all the stories in History,' wrote Jaime Gil, 'the saddest is no doubt Spain's, / because it ends badly.' Does it end badly? We'll never know who that militiaman was who spared Sánchez Mazas' life, nor what passed through his mind when he looked him in the eye; we'll never know what José and Manuel Machado said to each other before the graves of their brother Antonio and their mother. I don't know why, but sometimes I think, if we managed to unveil one of these parallel secrets, we might perhaps also touch on a much more essential secret.

I was very pleased with the article. When it was published, on 22 February 1999, exactly sixty years after Machado's death in Collioure, exactly sixty years and twenty-two days after Sánchez Mazas faced the firing squad at Collell (although the exact date of the execution I only learned later), my colleagues at the paper congratulated me. I received three letters over the following days; to my surprise – I've never been a polemical columnist, one of those names that abound in the letters to the editor, and there was nothing to suggest that events of sixty years ago could upset anyone very much – all three referred to the article. The first, which I imagined was written by a university student from the literature department, reproached me for having insinuated (something I don't think I did, or at least not entirely) in my article that, had Antonio Machado been in rebel Burgos in July of 1936, he would have taken Franco's side. The second was worse; it was written by a man old enough to have lived through the war. He accused me of 'revisionism' in unmistakable jargon, because the question in the last paragraph following the quote from Jaime Gil (Does it end badly?) suggested in a barely veiled way that Spain's story ends well, which in his judgement is completely false. 'It ends well for those who won the war,' he said. 'But badly for those of us who lost it. No one has ever even bothered to thank us for fighting for liberty. There is a monument to the war dead in every town in Spain. How many have you seen with, at the very least, the names of the fallen from both sides?' The letter finished: 'And damn the Transition! Sincerely, Mateu Recasens.'

The third letter was the most interesting. It was signed by someone called Miquel Aguirre. Aguirre was a historian and, according to what he said, had spent several years investigating what happened during the Civil War in the Banyoles region. Among other things, his letter gave details of a fact which at that moment struck me as astonishing: Sánchez Mazas hadn't been the only survivor of the Collell execution; a man named Jesús Pascual Aguilar also escaped with his life. Even more: it seemed Pascual had recounted the episode in a book called *I Was Murdered by the Reds*. 'I'm afraid this book is virtually unobtainable,' concluded the letter with the unmistakable petulance of the erudite. 'But if you are interested, I can place a copy at your disposal.' At the bottom of the letter Aguirre had put his address and a phone number.

I phoned the number immediately. After a few misunderstandings, from which I deduced that he worked for some sort of company or public institution, I managed to speak to Aguirre. I asked if he had information about the execution at Collell; he said yes. I asked if he was still willing to lend me Pascual's book; he said yes. I then asked if he'd like to meet for lunch; he said he lived in Banyoles, but came to Gerona every Thursday to record a radio programme.

'We could meet next Thursday,' he said.

It was Friday and, at the thought of a week's impatience, I was about to suggest we meet that very afternoon, in Banyoles.

'Okay,' I said, nevertheless. And at that moment I thought of Ferlosio with his innocent guru air and fiercely cheerful eyes, talking about his father on the terrace at the Bistrot. I asked: 'Shall we meet at the Bistrot?'

The Bistrot is a bar in the old part of the city, with a vaguely modernist feel to it, marble and wrought-iron tables,

14

rotary fans, its balconies brimming with flowers and over-looking the flight of steps leading up to the Sant Domènech Plaza. On Thursday, long before the time I'd agreed with Aguirre, I was seated at a table in the Bistrot with a beer in my hand; around me bubbled the conversations of the professors from the literature department who usually ate there. As I flipped through a magazine I thought how, making the lunch arrangements, it hadn't occurred to either Aguirre or I, since we'd never met, that one of us should have mentioned some way of recognizing each other, and I was just starting to try to imagine what Aguirre might look like, solely from the voice I'd heard over the phone a week before, when a short, stocky, dark-haired individual wearing glasses stopped in front of my table with a red folder under his arm, his face barely visible under three-days' growth of stubble and a bad-guy goatee. For some reason I'd expected Aguirre to be a calm, professorial old man, not this extremely young individual standing before me with a hung-over (or perhaps just eccentric) look to him. Since he didn't say anything, I asked him if he were him. He said yes. Then he asked me if I were me. I said yes. We laughed. When the waitress came, Aguirre ordered rice *à la cazuela* and an *entrecôte au roquefort*; I ordered the rabbit and a salad. While we waited for the food Aguirre told me he'd recognized me from a photo on the back of one of my books, which he'd read a while ago. Recovering from the initial spasm of vanity, I remarked grudgingly: 'Oh, you were the one, were you?'

'I don't understand.'

I felt obliged to clarify: 'It was a joke.'

I was anxious to get to the point, but, as I didn't want to

seem rude or overly interested, I asked him about the radio programme. Aguirre let out a nervous laugh, showing his teeth: white and uneven.

'It's supposed to be a humorous programme, but really it's just crap. I play a fascist police commissioner called Antonio Gargallo who prepares reports about the people he interrogates. The truth is I think I'm falling in love with him. Naturally, they know nothing about any of this at the Town Hall.'

'You work at Banyoles Town Hall?'

Aguirre nodded, looking half embarrassed and half sorrowful.

'Secretary to the mayor,' he said. 'More crap. The mayor's an old friend, he asked and I didn't know how to say no. But when this term finishes, I'm quitting.'

Since fairly recently, the municipal government of Banyoles had been in the hands of a team of very young members of the Catalan Republican Left, the radical nationalist party. Aguirre said:

'I don't know what you think, sir, but to me a civilized country is one where people don't have to waste their time on politics.'

I noticed the 'sir', but didn't let it bother me, and instead leapt to grasp the rope Aguirre had just thrown me, catching it in mid air: 'Just the opposite of what happened in '36.'

'Exactly.'

They brought the salad and the rice. Aguirre pointed at the red folder. 'I photocopied the Pascual book for you.'

'Do you know very much about what happened at Collell?'

'Not very much, no,' he said. 'It was a confusing episode.'

As he shovelled big forkfuls of rice into his mouth and washed them down with glasses of red wine, Aguirre told me, as if he felt he must put me in the picture, about the early days of the war in the region of Banyoles: the predictable failure of the coup d'état, the resulting revolution, the unconstrained savagery of the committees, the widespread burning of churches and massacres of the clergy.

'Even though it's not in style any more, I'm still anti-clerical – but that was collective madness,' he added. 'Of course, it's easy to find explanations for it, but it's also easy to find explanations for Nazism. Some nationalist historians insinuate that the ones who burned down churches and killed priests were from elsewhere – immigrants and suchlike. It's a lie: they were from here, and three years later more than one of them cheered the arrival of Franco's troops. Of course, if you ask, nobody was there when they torched the churches. But that's another story. What pisses me off are those nationalists who still go around trying to sell the nonsense that it was a war between Castilians and Catalans, a movie with good guys and bad guys.'

'I thought you were a nationalist.'

Aguirre stopped eating.

'I'm not a nationalist,' he said. 'I'm an *independentista*.'

'And what's the difference?'

'Nationalism is an ideology,' he explained, hardening his voice a little, as if annoyed at having to clarify the obvious. 'Insidious in my opinion. Independence is only a possibility. Since nationalism is a belief, and beliefs aren't up for debate, you can't argue about it; you can about independence. To you, sir, it may seem reasonable or not. To me it does.'

I couldn't take it any more.

'I'd prefer you not to call me sir.'

'Sorry,' he said, smiled and went back to his meal. 'I'm used to talking to older people respectfully.'

Aguirre kept talking about the war; he went into great detail about the final days when – the municipal and Generalitat governments having been inoperative for months – a stampede-like disorder reigned in the region: roads invaded by interminable caravans of refugees, soldiers in uniform of every rank wandering the countryside, desperate and driven to theft, enormous piles of weapons and equipment left in the ditches . . . Aguirre explained that at Collell, which had been used as a jail since the beginning of the war, there were close to a thousand prisoners being held at that time, and all or almost all of them came from Barcelona; they'd been moved there, ahead of the unstoppable advance of the rebel troops, because they were among the most dangerous or most involved in Franco's cause. Unlike Ferlosio, Aguirre did think the Republicans knew who they were executing, because the fifty they chose were very significant prisoners, people who were destined to occupy positions of social or political importance after the war: the provincial chief of the Falange in Barcelona, leaders of fifth-column groups, financiers, lawyers and priests, the majority of whom had been held in the *checas* in Barcelona and later on prison-ships like the *Argentina* and the *Uruguay*.

They brought the steak and the rabbit and took away the other plates (Aguirre's so clean it shone). I asked: 'Who gave the order?'

'What order?' Aguirre countered, eagerly surveying his

enormous sirloin, with steak knife and fork at the ready, about to attack.

'To have them shot.'

Aguirre regarded me for a moment as if he'd forgotten I was there across from him. He shrugged his shoulders and took a loud, deep breath.

'I don't know,' he answered, exhaling as he cut a piece of steak. 'I think Pascual insinuates that it was someone called Monroy, a tough young guy who might have run the prison, because in Barcelona he'd also run *checas* and work camps; he's mentioned in other testimonies from the time . . . In any case, if it *was* Monroy he most likely wasn't acting on his own volition, but obeying orders from the SIM.'

'The SIM?'

'The *Servicio de Información Militar*,' Aguirre clarified. 'One of the few army organizations that was still fully functioning by that stage.' He stopped chewing for a second, then went back to speaking with his mouth full: 'It's a reasonable hypothesis: it was a desperate moment, and the SIM, of course, wouldn't bother with small fry. But there are others.'

'For example?'

'Líster. He was around there. My father saw him.'

'At Collell.'

'In Sant Miquel de Campmajor, very near there. My father was a child then and they'd sent him to a farm in that village for safety. He's told me many times about one day when a handful of men burst into the farm, Líster amongst them; they demanded food and a place to sleep and spent the night arguing in the dining room. For a long time I thought this story was an invention of my father's, especially when I

19

realized the majority of old men who'd been alive then claimed to have seen Líster, an almost legendary character from the time he took command of the Fifth Regiment – but over the years I've been putting two and two together and I've come to the conclusion that it just might be true. You see,' he began, greedily soaking a piece of bread in the puddle of sauce his steak was swimming in (I thought he must've recovered from his hangover, and wondered if he wasn't enjoying the food more than the display of his knowledge of the war). 'Líster had just been made a colonel at the end of January '39. They'd put him in charge of the V Corps of the Army of the Ebro, or rather, what was left of the V Corps: a handful of shattered units barely putting up a fight, retreating in the direction of the French border. Líster's men were in the region for several weeks and some of them were definitely stationed at Collell. But as I was saying – have you read Líster's memoirs?'

I said I hadn't.

'Well, it's not exactly a memoir,' Aguirre went on. 'The book's called *Our War*, and it's pretty good, though he tells a tremendous number of lies, as in all memoirs. But the point is he writes that in February '39, on the night of the third to the morning of the fourth (or three days after the Collell execution), they held a meeting of the Politburo of the Communist Party at a farm in a nearby village, attended by, among other leaders and commissars, himself and Togliatti, who was then the Comintern delegate. If I'm not mistaken, they talked about the possibility of mounting a last-ditch resistance to the enemy in Catalonia at that meeting – but that doesn't matter: what counts is that the farm could well be the one where my father was staying as a refugee; at least the protagonists, the dates and places coincide, so . . .'

Then, without realizing it, Aguirre unwittingly got me entangled in a recondite, filial digression. I remember thinking of my father at that moment, and being surprised, because it had been a long time since I'd thought of him; I didn't know why, but there was a lump in my throat, like a shadow of guilt.

'So, it was Líster who gave the order to shoot them?' I interrupted.

'It could have been,' he said, readily picking up the lost thread while scraping his plate clean. 'But it could just as easily not have been. In *Our War* he says it wasn't him, not him or his men. What else is he going to say? But, the fact is, I believe him – it wasn't his style, he was too obsessed with continuing by whatever means possible a war he'd already lost. Besides, half the things they attribute to Líster are pure legend, and the other half . . . well, I guess they're true. But who knows? What seems beyond doubt to me is that whoever gave that order knew perfectly well who they were executing and, of course, who Sánchez Mazas was. Mmm,' he moaned, wiping up the last of the roquefort sauce with a piece of bread, 'I was so hungry! Do you want a bit more wine?'

They took the plates away (mine with abundant remains of rabbit; Aguirre's again so clean it shone). He ordered another carafe of wine, a piece of chocolate cake and coffee; I ordered coffee. I asked Aguirre what he knew about Sánchez Mazas and his stay at Collell.

'Not much,' he answered. 'His name appears a couple of times in the General Prosecution Records, but always in relation to his trial in Barcelona, when they caught him after

21

he escaped from Madrid. Pascual also mentions him once or twice too. As far as I know the only one who might know more is Trapiello, Andrés Trapiello. The writer. He's edited Sánchez Mazas and written some really good things about him; he's always mentioning Sánchez Mazas' family in his diaries, so he must be in contact with them. I think I may even have read an account of the firing squad incident in one of his books . . . It's a story that circulated extensively after the war, everyone who knew Sánchez Mazas then used to tell it, I suppose because he used to tell everyone. Did you know lots of people thought it was a lie? In fact, there still are those who think so.'

'Doesn't surprise me.'

'Why not?'

'Because it sounds like fiction.'

'All wars are full of stories that sound like fiction.'

'Yeah, but doesn't it still seem incredible that a man who's not particularly young, forty-five years old by then, and extremely short-sighted . . . ?'

'Well, of course. And who would have been in a pitiful state besides.'

'Exactly. Doesn't it seem incredible that a guy like that could manage to escape from such a situation?'

'But why incredible?' The arrival of the wine, cake and coffees didn't interrupt his reasoning. 'Surprising, yes. But not incredible. But you explained all that so well in your article! Remember it was a firing squad *en masse*. Remember the soldier who had to turn him in and didn't. And remember we're talking about Collell. Have you ever been there?'

I told him I hadn't, and Aguirre began to describe an

enormous mass of stone besieged by thick pine forests on limy soil, a vast, mountainous, rough territory, scattered with isolated farms and tiny villages (Torn, Sant Miquel de Campmajor, Fares, Sant Ferriol, Mieres); during the war years numerous escape networks operated in these villages that, in exchange for money (sometimes out of friendship or even political affinities), helped potential victims of revolutionary repression to cross the border, as well as young men of military age who wanted to evade the compulsory conscription ordered by the Republic. According to Aguirre, the area was seething with runaways as well, people who couldn't afford the expenses of escape or didn't manage to make contact with the networks, and stayed under cover in the woods for months or even years.

'So it was the ideal place to hide,' he argued. 'By that point in the war the locals were used to dealing with fugitives, helping them out. Did Ferlosio tell you about the "forest friends"?'

My article finished at the moment the militiaman didn't give Sánchez Mazas away, not a word about the 'forest friends'. I choked on my coffee.

'Do you know about them?' I inquired.

'I know the son of one of them.'

'You're kidding.'

'I'm not kidding. He's called Jaume Figueras, he lives right near here. In Cornellà de Terri.'

'Ferlosio told me the lads who helped Sánchez Mazas were from Cornellà de Terri.'

Aguirre shrugged his shoulders as he picked up the last crumbs of chocolate cake with his fingers.

'You know more than I do then,' he admitted. 'Figueras just told me the gist of the story; but then I wasn't all that interested. I could give you his phone number and you can ask him yourself.'

Aguirre finished his coffee and we paid. We said goodbye on the Rambla, in front of Les Peixeteries Velles Bridge. Aguirre said he'd call me the following day to give me Figueras' phone number and, as we shook hands, I noticed two smudges of chocolate darkening the corners of his mouth.

'What are you thinking of doing with this?' he asked.

I was verging on telling him to wipe his lips.

'With what?' I said, instead.

'With the Sánchez Mazas story.'

I wasn't thinking of doing anything with it – I was simply curious about it – so I told him the truth.

'Nothing?' Aguirre looked at me with his small, nervous, intelligent eyes. 'I thought you were thinking of writing a novel.'

'I don't write novels anymore,' I said. 'Besides, it's not a novel, it's a true story.'

'So was the article,' said Aguirre. 'Did I tell you how much I liked it? I liked it because it was like a compressed tale, except with real characters and situations . . . Like a true tale.'

The next day Aguirre called me and gave me Jaume Figueras' phone number. It was a mobile number. Figueras didn't answer, but his voice did, asking me to record a message, so I did: I said my name, my profession, that I knew Aguirre, that I was interested in talking to him about his father, Sánchez Mazas, and the 'forest friends'; I also left my phone number and asked him to call me.

For the next few days I anxiously awaited a call from Figueras, which didn't come. I called him again, I left another message, and went back to waiting. In the meantime I read *I was Murdered by the Reds*, Pascual Aguilar's book. It was a truculent reminder of the horrors experienced behind Republican lines, just another of the many that appeared in Spain when the war ended, except this one had been published in September 1981. The date, I fear, is not coincidental, for it can be read as both a sort of justification of those involved in the comic-opera coup on 23 February of that year (Pascual quotes several times a revealing phrase that José Antonio Primo de Rivera used to repeat as if it were his own: 'At the eleventh hour it has always been a squad of soldiers that has saved civilization'), and as a warning of the catastrophes to come with the imminent rise of the Socialist Party to power and the symbolic finale of the Transition; surprisingly, the book is very good. Pascual, who'd not had a single one of his 'old shirt' Falangist convictions eroded either by time or the changes that had occurred in Spain, nimbly recounts his adventures during the war, from the moment the military uprising catches him on vacation in a village in Teruel, which falls in the Republican zone, up to a few days after facing the firing squad in Collell – to which he dedicates many pages and fierce attention to detail, including the preceding and following days – when he's liberated by Franco's army, after having spent the war leading the life of a combination of the Scarlet Pimpernel and Henri de Lagardère, first as an active member and later as leader of a Barcelona fifth-column group, and having spent time locked up in the Vallmajor *checa*. Pascual's book was self-published; it contains several references to

Sánchez Mazas, with whom Pascual spent the hours leading up to the execution. Following Aguirre's suggestion, I likewise read Trapiello, and in one of his books discovered that he too told the story of Sánchez Mazas facing the firing squad, and in almost the exact same way I'd heard Ferlosio tell it, except for the fact that, like me in my article or my true tale, he didn't mention the 'forest friends' either. The exact similarity between Trapiello's tale and mine surprised me. I thought Trapiello must have heard it from Ferlosio (or one of Sánchez Mazas' other children, or his wife) and imagined that, having been told so often by Sánchez Mazas in his house, it must have acquired for the family an almost formulaic character, like those perfect comic stories where you can't leave out a single word without spoiling the joke.

I got hold of Trapiello's phone number and called him in Madrid. As soon as I revealed the reason for my call he was very friendly and, although he said it had been years since he'd dealt with Sánchez Mazas, he seemed thrilled that someone was taking an interest in him; I suspected that he didn't consider Sánchez Mazas a good writer, but a great writer. Our conversation lasted over an hour. Trapiello assured me he knew no more about the Collell incident than what he'd written in his book and confirmed that, especially just after the war, many people recounted it.

'It used to turn up quite often in the Barcelona newspapers just after Catalonia was occupied by Franco's troops, and in those of the rest of the country, because it was one of the last outbursts of violence in the Catalan rearguard and they had to take full advantage of it for propaganda,' Trapiello explained. 'If I'm not mistaken, Ridruejo mentions the incident in his memoirs, and so does Laín. And I must have a Montes article somewhere that also talks about it . . . I imagine that for a time Sánchez Mazas went around telling everyone he came across. Obviously it's a brutal story, but, well, I don't know . . . I suppose he was such a coward (and everyone knew he was such a coward) that he must have thought this tremendous episode redeemed his cowardice in some way.'

I asked him if he'd heard anything about the 'forest friends'. He said he had. I asked who had told him the story he told in his book. He said Liliana Ferlosio, Sánchez Mazas' wife, whom it seemed he'd visited frequently before her death.

'It's odd,' I remarked. 'Except for one detail, the story coincides point by point with what Ferlosio told me – as if, instead of telling it, they'd both recited it.'

'Which detail is that?'

'A minor one. In your telling (in Liliana's, that is), when he sees Sánchez Mazas the militiaman shrugs his shoulders and then he walks away. In mine (in Ferlosio's, that is), before he leaves the militiaman looks him in the eye for a few seconds.'

There was a silence. I thought the line had gone dead. 'Hello?'

'It's funny,' Trapiello reflected. 'Now that you mention it, that's true. I don't know where I got the shrug of the shoulders, it must have struck me as more dramatic, or more like Pío Baroja. I think, in fact, Liliana told me the militiaman stared him in the eye before he left. Yes. I even remember her saying one time, when she was reunited with Sánchez Mazas after the three years of separation during the war, he often used to talk to her about those eyes that had stared at him. The militiaman's eyes, I mean.'

Before we hung up we talked a bit more about Sánchez Mazas, about his poetry and his novels and articles, his difficult personality, his friendships and his family ('In that house everyone speaks badly about everyone else, and they're all right,' Trapiello told me González-Ruano used to say). As if he took it for granted that I was going to write something about Sánchez Mazas, but out of some scruple of decency didn't want to ask me what, Trapiello gave me a few names and some bibliographic leads and invited me to come and see him in Madrid, where he had manuscripts and photocopies of newspaper articles and other things by Sánchez Mazas.

I didn't visit Trapiello until several months later, but I immediately began to follow up the leads he'd provided. That's how I discovered that, especially right after the end of the war, Sánchez Mazas had indeed told everyone who'd listen the story of his firing squad experience. Eugenio Montes, one of the most faithful friends he had (a writer like him, like him a Falangist), on 14 February 1939, just two weeks after the events at Collell, described him 'in a shepherd's jacket and bullet-ridden trousers', arriving 'almost resurrected from the other world' after three years of hiding and jail cells in the Republican zone. Sánchez Mazas and Montes had been joyfully reunited a few days earlier in Barcelona, in the office of the then National Chief of Propaganda for the rebels, the poet Dionisio Ridruejo. Many years later, in his memoirs, he still recalled the scene, just as another illustrious young Falangist hierarch of the moment, Pedro Laín Entralgo, did in his, somewhat later. The descriptions the two memoir writers give of Sánchez Mazas – whom Ridruejo knew a little, but whom Laín, later to loathe him, had never seen before – are noticeably similar, as if they'd been so impressed that memory had frozen the image in a common snapshot (or as if Laín had copied Ridruejo; or they'd both copied the same source): for them too he had a resurrected air, skinny, nervous and disconcerted, his hair cropped close and his curved nose dominating the famished face; they both also remember Sánchez Mazas telling the firing squad story in that very office, but perhaps Ridruejo didn't entirely believe him (and thus mentioned the 'rather novelistic details' with which he adorned the tale for them); and only Laín hadn't forgotten he was wearing a 'rough, dark sheepskin'.

Because, as I found out by chance and, after a few unusually simple procedures, was able to verify sitting in a cubicle of the Catalan Filmoteca archives, Sánchez Mazas in that same rough dark sheepskin and with that same resurrected air – skinny and with close-cropped hair – also told his firing squad story in front of a camera, undoubtedly around the same time in February 1939 when he'd told his Falangist comrades in Ridruejo's office in Barcelona. The film – one of the few remaining of Sánchez Mazas – appeared in one of the first post-war news broadcasts, among martial images of Generalísimo Franco reviewing the Armada at Tarragona and idyllic images of Carmencita Franco playing in the garden of their residence in Burgos with a lion cub, a gift from Social Welfare. Sánchez Mazas is standing throughout, not wearing his glasses, his gaze a little lost; he speaks, however, with the aplomb of a man accustomed to doing so in public, with the pleasure of someone who enjoys the sound of his own voice, in a tone strangely ironic at first – when he alludes to the execution – and predictably exalted at the conclusion – when he alludes to the end of his odyssey – always a bit bombastic, but his words are so precise and the silences which govern them so measured, that he too at times gives the impression that instead of telling the story he's reciting it, like an actor playing his part on stage; otherwise, the story doesn't differ substantially from the one his son recounted to me . . . So as I listened to him tell it, sitting on a stool in front of a video player, in a Filmoteca cubicle, I couldn't suppress a vague tremor, because I knew I was hearing one of the first versions, still rough and unpolished, of the same story Ferlosio was to tell me almost sixty years later, and I felt absolutely sure that what Sánchez Mazas had told his son (and what he'd told me) wasn't what he remembered happening, but what he remembered having told before. Also I wasn't in the least surprised that neither Montes nor Ridruejo nor Laín (supposing they even knew of his existence), nor of course Sánchez Mazas himself in that news bulletin directed at a numerous and anonymous mass of spectators relieved by the recent end of the war, mentioned the gesture of that nameless soldier who had orders to kill him and did not kill him; the fact is understandable without need to attribute forgetfulness or ingratitude to anyone: suffice to remember that the doctrine of war in Franco's Spain, as in all wars, dictated that no enemy had ever saved anyone's life: they were too busy taking them. And as for the 'forest friends' . . .

A few more months passed before I managed to speak to Jaume Figueras. After leaving several messages on his mobile phone and not receiving a single reply to any of them, I had almost given up hope that he'd get in touch with me, and on occasion surmised that he must be only a figment of Aguirre's overwrought imagination – or, for reasons unknown but not difficult to imagine, that Figueras simply did not welcome the idea of recalling for anyone his father's wartime adventure. What is odd (or at least it strikes me as odd now) is that in all the time since Ferlosio's tale first awoke my curiosity, it never occurred to me that any of the story's protagonists could still be alive, as if the event had happened not a mere sixty years ago, but was as remote in time as the battle of Salamis.

One day I chanced to run into Aguirre. It was in a Mexican restaurant where I'd gone to interview a nauseating novelist from Madrid who was in the city promoting his latest flatulence, which took place in Mexico; Aguirre was with a group of people, celebrating something I imagine, as I can still remember their loud, jubilant laughter and his tequila breath hitting me in the face. He came over and, nervously stroking his bad-guy goatee, asked me point-blank whether I was writing (which meant whether I was writing a book: like almost everyone, Aguirre didn't consider writing for a newspaper actual writing); a little annoyed, because nothing irritates a writer who doesn't write as much as being asked about what he's writing, I said no. He asked me what had happened with Sánchez Mazas and my true tale; even more annoyed, I said: nothing. Then he asked me if I'd spoken to Figueras. I must have been a bit drunk too, or maybe the nauseating novelist from Madrid had already got me worked up, because I said no, and petulantly added:

'If he even exists.'

'If who even exists?'

'Who do you think? Figueras.'

The comment wiped the smile off his face; he stopped stroking his goatee.

'Don't be an idiot,' he said, focusing his astonished eyes on me, and I felt a tremendous urge to slap him, though probably it was really the novelist from Madrid I wanted to slap. 'Of course he exists.'

I restrained myself.

'Then he doesn't want to talk to me.'

Almost remorseful, almost excusing himself, Aguirre explained that Figueras was a builder or contractor (or something like that) as well as a town planning advisor (or something like that) in Cornellà de Terri, that he was, in any case, a very busy person and that undoubtedly explained why he hadn't responded to my messages; then he promised he'd speak to him. When I went back to my seat I felt awful: heart and soul I despised the novelist from Madrid, who was still holding forth.

Three days later Figueras called me. He apologized for not having done so sooner (his voice sounded slow and distant on the phone, as if the man it belonged to were very elderly, perhaps unwell), he mentioned Aguirre, then asked me if I still wanted to talk to him. I said yes; but arranging a date wasn't easy. Finally, after going through every day of the week, we decided on the following week; and after going through every bar in town (beginning with the Bistrot which Figueras didn't know), we settled on the Núria, in the plaza Poeta Marquina, very close to the station.

There I was a week later, almost a quarter of an hour before the time we'd agreed. I remember the afternoon very clearly because the following day I was going on holiday to Cancún, in Mexico, with a girlfriend I'd been seeing for a while (the third since my separation: the first was a colleague from the newspaper; the second, a girl who worked at a Pans and Company sandwich shop). Her name was Conchi and her only job I knew of was that of fortune-teller on the local television station; her stage name was Jasmine. Conchi intimidated me a little, but I suspect I've always liked women who intimidate me a little, and obviously I made sure no acquaintance would surprise me with her – not so much because I was embarrassed to be seen dating a well-known fortune-teller, as for her rather flashy appearance (bleached blonde hair, leather mini-skirt, tight tops and spike heels); and also because, why lie, Conchi was a little bit special. I remember the first time I took her back to my place. While I was wrestling with the lock on the main door, she said:

'This city's fucking pathetic.'

I asked her why.

'Look,' she said and, with a grimace of utter disgust, pointed to a plaque which read: 'Avinguda Lluís Pericot. Prehistorian.' 'They could've named the street after someone who'd at least finished university, don't you think?'

Conchi loved the idea of dating a journalist (an intellectual, she'd say) and, although I'm sure she never finished reading a single one of my articles (or only the odd very short one), she always pretended to read them and in the place of honour in her living room, flanking an image of the Virgin of Guadalupe raised up on a pedestal, she had a copy of each of my books exquisitely sheathed in clear plastic. 'He's my boyfriend,' I imagined her telling her semiliterate friends, feeling very superior to them, each time one stepped into her house. When

I met her, Conchi had just split up with an Ecuadorian called Dos-a-Dos González, whose name, it seemed, had been chosen in honour of a football match when the team his father had supported for his entire lifetime won their national league for the first and only time. To get over Dos-a-Dos – whom she'd met at a gym, body-building, and who in good times she affectionately called Two-All and in bad ones, Brains, Brains González – Conchi had moved to Quart, a town near by, where, almost in the middle of a forest, she'd rented a great big ramshackle house very cheaply. In a subtle but insistent way, I kept telling her to move back to the city, and my insistence was based on two lines of reasoning: one explicit and another implicit, one public and another secret. The public one was that the isolated house was a danger for her, but the day two individuals attempted to break in and Conchi, who unfortunately was home at the time, ended up chasing them through the woods throwing stones at them, I had to admit that the house was a danger for anyone who tried to break into it. The secret reason was that, since I didn't have a driver's licence, every time we went from my house to Conchi's house or from Conchi's house to my house, we had to go in Conchi's Volkswagen, a wreck so old it could well merit the attention of the prehistorian Pericot and which Conchi always drove as if she might still be in time to prevent an imminent break-in at her house, and as if all the cars moving around us were occupied by an army of delinquents. So, any car journey with my girlfriend, who needless to say loved to drive, entailed a gamble I was only willing to undertake in very exceptional circumstances; these must have occurred fairly often, at least at the beginning, because I risked my neck quite a few times back then going from her house to mine or my house to hers in her Volkswagen. Moreover, although I fear I wasn't willing to admit it, I think I liked Conchi a lot (more in any case than my colleague at the newspaper and the girl from Pans and Company; less, perhaps, than my former wife); enough, in any case, that to celebrate going out together for nine months I let her convince me to spend two weeks in Cancún, a place I imagined as truly frightful, but which (I hoped) the pleasure of being with Conchi and her amazing cheerfulness would render at least tolerable. So the evening I finally managed to arrange to meet Figueras I was already packed and impatient to be off on a trip that I sometimes (but only sometimes) considered rash.

I sat down at a table in the Núria, ordered a gin and tonic and waited. It wasn't eight o'clock yet; in front of me, on the other side of the glass walls, the terrace was full of people and beyond them every once in a while a commuter train went by on the viaduct. To my left, in the park, children accompanied by their mothers played on the swings, under the sloping shadows of the plane trees. I remember I thought of Conchi, who not long before had surprised me by saying she wasn't planning to go to her grave childless, and of my former wife, who many years before had judiciously refused my suggestion that we have a child. I thought if Conchi's declaration had also been a hint (and I now think I understand that it was), then the trip to Cancún was doubly ill-advised, because I now had no intention of ever having a child; the idea of having one with Conchi struck me as laughable. For some reason I thought of my father again, and I felt guilty again. 'Soon,' I surprised myself thinking, 'when even I don't remember him, he'll be completely dead.' At that moment, as I saw a man in his sixties come into the bar, who I thought could be Figueras, I cursed myself for having arranged two meetings with strangers, in just a few months, without previously agreeing on a way to recognize each other: I stood up, asked him if he were Jaume Figueras; he said no. I went back to my table: it was almost eight-thirty. I looked around the bar for a man on his own; then I went out to the terrace, also in vain. I wondered if Figueras had been in the bar all that time, near me and, fed up with waiting, had left; I decided that it was impossible. I didn't have his mobile number with me, so, choosing to believe that for some reason Figueras was running late and was about to arrive, I opted to wait. I ordered another gin and tonic and sat down at a table on the terrace. I nervously watched the tables around me and those inside; while I was doing so, two young Gypsies came up – a man and a woman – with an electric keyboard, a microphone and a speaker, and started playing for the customers. The man played and the woman sang. They played mostly paso dobles: I remember very well because Conchi loved paso dobles so much that she'd tried unsuccessfully to get me to sign up for a course to learn how to dance them, and especially because it was the first time in my life I heard the lyrics to 'Sighing for Spain', a very famous paso doble I didn't even know had lyrics:

> God desired, in his power,
> to blend four little sunbeams
> and make of them a woman
> and when His will was done

in a Spanish garden I was born
like a flower on her rose-bush.
Glorious land of my love,
blessed land of perfume and passion,
Spain, in each flower at your feet
a heart is sighing.
Oh, I'm dying of sorrow,
for I'm going away, Spain, from you,
for away from my rose-bush I'm torn.*

Listening to the Gypsies play and sing I thought it was the saddest song in the world; also, barely admitting it to myself, that I wouldn't mind dancing to it one day. When they finished their act, I tossed a hundred pesetas in the Gypsy woman's hat and, as the people started leaving the terrace, I finished off my gin and tonic and left.

When I got home I had a message on my answering machine from Figueras. He apologized and said something unexpected had arisen at the last minute and kept him from turning up to meet me; he asked me to call him. I called him. He apologized again and suggested another meeting.

'I have something for you,' he added.

'What?'

'I'll give it to you when we see each other.'

I told him I was going on holiday the following day (I was embarrassed to tell him I was going to Cancún) and wouldn't

---

* Quiso Dios, con su poder,/ fundir cuatro rayitos de sol/ y hacer con ellos una mujer,/ y al cumplir su voluntad/ en un jardín de España nací/ como la flor en el rosal./ Tierra gloriosa de mi querer,/ tierra bendita de perfume y pasión,/ España, en toda flor a tus pies/ suspira un corazón./ Ay de mi pena mortal,/ porque me alejo, España, de ti,/ porque me arrancan de mi rosal.

37

be back for a fortnight. We arranged to meet in the Núria in two weeks' time and, after going through the idiotic exercise of superficially describing ourselves to each other, said goodbye.

The Cancún thing was unspeakable. Conchi, who'd organized the trip, had hidden the fact that, except for a couple of excursions into the Yucatán peninsula and many afternoon shopping trips to the city centre, the whole thing amounted to spending two weeks trapped in a hotel with a gang of Catalans, Andalusians and North Americans ruled by a whistle-wielding tour guide and two monitors who had no understanding of the concept of rest and spoke not a word of Spanish; I'd be lying if I denied it had been years since I'd been so happy. And strange as it may seem, I believe without the stay in Cancún (or in a hotel in Cancún) I'd never have decided to write a book about Sánchez Mazas, because over the course of those days I had time to put my ideas about him in order and came to realize that the character and his story had over time turned into one of those obsessions that constitute the indispensable fuel for writing. Sitting on the balcony of my room with a *mojito* in hand, while watching how Conchi and her gang of Catalans, Andalusians and North Americans were relentlessly pursued, the length and breadth of the hotel, by the fury of the sports monitors ('Now, swimming-pool!'), I couldn't stop thinking about Sánchez Mazas. I soon arrived at a conclusion: the more I knew about him, the less I understood him; the less I understood him, the more he intrigued me; the more he intrigued me, the more I wanted to know about him. I had known – but not understood and was intrigued – that cultured, refined, melancholic and conservative man, bereft of physical courage and allergic to violence, undoubtedly because he knew himself incapable of exercising it, had worked during the twenties and thirties harder than almost anyone so that his country would be submerged in a savage orgy of blood. I don't know who it was who said: no matter who wins a war, the poets always lose. I do know that, just before my vacation in Cancún, I'd read that, on 29 October 1933, in the first public act of the Spanish Falange in the Madrid Drama Theatre, José Antonio Primo de Rivera, who was always surrounded by poets, had said 'people have never been moved except by their poets'. The first statement is stupid, not the second: it's true that wars are made for money, which is power, but young men go off to the front and kill and get killed for words, which are poetry, and that's why poets are always the ones who win wars; and for this reason Sánchez Mazas – who from his position of privilege at José Antonio's side contrived a violent patriotic poetry of sacrifice and yokes and arrows and the usual cries that inflamed the imaginations of hundreds of youths and would eventually send them to slaughter – is more responsible for the victory of Francoist arms than all the inept military man- oeuvres of that nineteenth-century general who was Francisco Franco. I'd known – but not understood and was intrigued – that, at the end of the war he had contributed more than almost anyone to starting, Franco had named him to a ministerial post in the first government of the Victory, but after a very short time had dismissed him because, rumour has it, he didn't even show up to the cabinet meetings and that from then on Sánchez Mazas abandoned active politics almost entirely and, as if he felt satisfied with the regime of grief he'd helped install in Spain and considered his work to be done, devoting the last twenty years of his life to writing, squandering his inheritance and filling his extensive leisure hours with rather extravagant hobbies. I was intrigued by that final era of retirement and peevishness, but most of all by the three war years, with their inextricable peripeteia, astonishing execution, militiaman saviour and forest friends, so one evening in Cancún (or in a Cancún hotel), as I whiled away the time before supper in the bar, I decided that, after almost ten years without writing a book, the moment to try again had arrived, and I also decided that the book I'd write would not be a novel, but simply a true tale, a tale cut from the cloth of reality, concocted out of true events and characters, a tale centred on Sánchez Mazas and the firing squad and the circumstances leading up to and following it.

Back from Cancún, I went to the Núria on the agreed evening to meet Figueras and arrived early as usual but hadn't yet ordered my gin and tonic when I was approached by a solid, stoop-shouldered man in his early fifties, with curly hair, deep blue eyes, and a modest rural smile. It was Jaume Figueras. Doubtless because I'd expected a much older man (as with Aguirre), I thought: The telephone puts on years. He ordered a coffee; I ordered a gin and tonic. Figueras apologized for not having shown up last time and for not being able to stay long this time. He explained that work piled up at that time of year and since he'd also put Cam Pigem, the family house in Cornellà de Terri, up for sale, he was very busy putting his father's papers in order; his father had died ten years ago. At this point Figueras' voice broke: with a moist glimmer sparkling in his eyes, he swallowed, then smiled as if apologizing again. The waiter relieved the awkward silence by bringing the coffee and gin and tonic. Figueras took a sip of coffee.

'Is it true you're going to write about my father and Sánchez Mazas?' he sprung on me.

'Who told you that?'

'Miquel Aguirre.'

A true tale, I thought, but didn't say. That's what I'm going to write. It also occurred to me that Figueras was thinking if someone wrote about his father, his father wouldn't be entirely dead. Figueras insisted:

'I might,' I lied. 'I don't know yet. Did your father often tell you about how he met Sánchez Mazas?'

Figueras said yes. He admitted though that he had no more than a vague knowledge of the facts.

'You have to understand,' he apologized again. 'It was just one of those family stories. I heard my father tell it so many times . . . At home, in the bar, on his own with us or surrounded by people from the village, because we had a bar in Cam Pigem for years. Anyway. I don't think I ever paid much attention. And now I regret it.'

What Figueras knew was that his father had fought the whole war for the Republic, and that when he came home, towards the end, he'd met up with his younger brother, Joaquim, and a friend of his, called Daniel Angelats, who had just deserted from the Republican ranks. He also knew that, since none of the three soldiers wanted to go into exile with the defeated army, they decided to await the imminent arrival of Franco's troops hidden in a nearby forest, and one day they saw a half-blind man groping his way towards them through the undergrowth. They stopped him at gunpoint;

41

they demanded he identify himself: the man said his name was Rafael Sánchez Mazas and that he was the most senior Falangist in Spain.

'My father knew who he was straightaway,' said Jaume Figueras. 'He was very well-read, he'd seen photos of Sánchez Mazas in the newspaper and had read his articles. Or at least that's what he always said. I don't know if it was true.'

'It could be,' I conceded. 'And then what happened?'

'They spent a few days hiding in the woods,' Figueras went on, after drinking the rest of his coffee. 'The four of them. Until the Nationalists arrived.'

'Didn't your father tell you what he talked about with Sánchez Mazas during the days they spent in the forest?'

'I suppose he must have,' Figueras answered. 'But I don't remember. Like I told you, I didn't pay much attention to those things. The only thing I remember is that Sánchez Mazas told them about the firing squad at Collell. You know the story, right?'

I nodded.

'He told them lots of other things too, that's for sure,' Figueras continued. 'My father always said that over the course of those days he and Sánchez Mazas became good friends.'

Figueras knew that, after the war, his father had been in prison, and that his family had begged him many times in vain to write to Sánchez Mazas, who was then a Minister, to ask him to intercede on his behalf. He also knew that once his father had got out of jail, he heard that someone from his village or from a village nearby, aware of the bonds of friendship between them, had written a letter to Sánchez Mazas in which he'd claimed to be one of the forest friends, and requested a gift of money as payment for the war debt, and that his father had written to Sánchez Mazas denouncing the impostor.

'Did Sánchez Mazas reply?'

'I think so, but I'm not sure. I haven't found any letters from him among my father's papers so far, and I shouldn't think he'd have thrown them away, he was a very careful man, he kept everything. I don't know, maybe they got misplaced, or maybe they'll turn up one of these days.' Figueras put his hand in his shirt pocket: slowly and deliberately. 'What I did find was this.'

He handed me a small, old notebook, with blackened oilcloth covers which had once been green. I leafed through it. Most of it was blank, but several of the first and last pages were scribbled on in pencil, with hurried but not entirely illegible handwriting that barely stood out against the dirty cream-coloured, squared paper; my first glance through it also revealed that several pages had been torn out.

'What's this?' I asked.

'The diary Sánchez Mazas had with him when he was in hiding in the forest,' Figueras replied. 'Or that's what it looks like. Keep it; but don't lose it, it's like a family heirloom, my father was very attached to it.' He looked at his wristwatch, tutted to himself and said: 'Well, I have to be off now. But call me another day.'

As he stood up, leaning his thick callused fingers on the table, he added:

'If you want I can show you the place in the woods where

they hid, the Mas de la Casa Nova; it's just a half-ruined farm nowadays, but if you're going to tell the story you'll want to see it. Of course if you're not thinking of telling it . . .'

'I still don't know what I'll do,' I lied again, caressing the oilcloth covers of the notebook, which burned in my hands like a treasure. With the aim of spurring Figueras' memory, I added quite honestly: 'But, the truth is, I thought you'd have more to tell me.'

'I've told you all I know,' he apologized for the umpteenth time – but now I seemed to glimpse a touch of guile or distrust on the watery surface of his blue eyes. 'Anyway, if you do plan to write about Sánchez Mazas and my father, you should really talk to my uncle. He definitely knows all the details.'

'What uncle?'

'My uncle Joaquim.' He explained: 'My father's brother. Another one of the forest friends.'

Incredulous, as if he'd just announced the resurrection of one of the soldiers of Salamis, I asked:

'He's alive?'

'I should think so!' Figueras laughed uneasily, and an artificial hand gesture made me think he was only pretending to be surprised at my surprise. 'Didn't I tell you? He lives in Medinyà but he spends a lot of time at the seaside in Montgó, and in Oslo too, because his son works there, for the WHO. I don't think you'll find him now, but in September I'm sure he'll be delighted to talk to you. Do you want me to suggest it to him?'

Slightly stunned by the news, I said of course I would.

'While I'm at it I'll see if I can find out Angelats' whereabouts,' said Figueras not hiding his satisfaction. 'He used to live in Banyoles, and he's probably still alive. Someone who definitely is, is Maria Ferré.'

'Who's Maria Ferré?'

Figueras visibly suppressed the urge to dig out an explanation.

'I'll tell you another time,' he said after looking at his watch again; then he held out his hand. 'I have to go now. I'll call you when I've arranged something with my uncle. He'll tell you everything, chapter and verse. He's got a very good memory; you'll see. Meanwhile, have a look at the notebook, I think it'll be of interest.'

I watched him pay, leave the Núria, get into a dusty jeep, carelessly parked at the entrance to the bar, and drive away. I stroked the notebook, but didn't open it. I finished drinking my gin and tonic and as I was getting up to go, saw an intercity train cross the viaduct behind the terrace full of people, and I thought of the Gypsies playing paso dobles two weeks ago in the tired light of an evening like this one and, when I got home and started to examine the notebook Figueras had entrusted to me, I'd still not disentangled the hauntingly sad melody of 'Sighing for Spain' from my memory.

I spent the night mulling over the notebook. In the first part it contained, after a few torn-out pages, a short diary written in pencil. Making an effort to decipher the handwriting, I read:

. . . settled by forest house – Food – Slept hayloft – Soldiers passed.

3- Day in Forest – Conversation old man – Doesn't dare have me in house – Forest – Build shelter.

4- Fall of Gerona – Conversation by fireside with fugitives – Old man treats me better than his wife does.

5- Waiting all day – stay hidden – Cannon fire.

6- Meet three lads in forest – Night – Vigilance [*illegible word*] shelter – Bridges blown up – The reds are leaving.

7- Meet the three lads in the morning – Modest lunch from what friends had.

The diary stops there. At the end of the notebook, after more torn out pages, written in different handwriting, but also in pencil, are the names of the three lads, the forest friends:

Pedro Figueras Bahí
Joaquín Figueras Bahí
Daniel Angelats Dilmé

And further down:

Casa Pigem de Cornellà
(across from the station)

Further down are the signatures, in ink – not pencil, like the rest of the writing in the book – of the two Figueras brothers, and on the following page is written:

Palol de Rebardit
Casa Borrell
Ferré Family

Instalado casa bosque
Comida – dormir pasado
por soldados –

3 – Día bosque – conversación
viejo – no se atreve a salir
... en casa – Bosque –
fabricación del refugio

4 – Caída de Germán – Conversación junto al ...
con los fugitivos – el
viejo me trata mejor –
por señora

5 – Día de espera – último
... refugio – Cañones

6 – Encuentro en el
bosque con los ...
...
...
los voy... se van

On another page, also in pencil and in the same handwriting as the diary, except much clearer, is the longest text in the notebook. It says:

I, Rafael Sánchez Mazas, founding member of the Spanish Falange, national adviser, ex-president of the Leadership Council and at present the senior Falangist in Spain and highest ranking in red territory, hereby declare:

1. that on the 30th of January 1939 I faced a firing squad at the Collell prison camp with 48 other unhappy prisoners and escaped miraculously after the first two rounds, breaking away into the forest –

2. that after three days' march through the forest, walking at night and asking for charity at the farms, I arrived in the area of Palol de Rebardit, where I fell into an irrigation ditch and lost my spectacles, leaving me half blind . . .

There's a page missing here, which has been torn out. But the text goes on:

. . . proximity of front line kept me hidden in their house until the Nationalist troops arrived.

4. that despite the generous objection of the inhabitants of the Borrell farm I wish by means of this document to confirm my promise to repay them with a substantial monetary reward, proposing the proprietor [here there is a blank space] for an honorary distinction if the military command is in agreement and to swear my immense and eternal gratitude to him and his family, all of which will be very little in comparison to what he has done for me.

Signed in the Casanova de un Pla farm near Cornellà de Terri at 1 . . .

That was the contents of the notebook. I reread it several times, trying to give those dispersed notes a coherent meaning, and link them to the facts I knew. To begin with, I discarded the suspicion, which insidiously crossed my mind as I read, that the notebook was a fraud, a falsification contrived by the Figueras family to deceive me, or to deceive someone: at the time I thought it didn't make much sense that a modest rural family would concoct so sophisticated a scheme. So sophisticated and, most of all, so absurd. Because, when Sánchez Mazas was alive, when it could have been a shield for defeated people against the reprisals of the victors, the document could easily have been authenticated and, once he was dead, it lost its value. Nevertheless, I thought that it would be a good idea to make sure the handwriting in the notebook (or one of the handwritings in the notebook, because there were several) and that of Sánchez Mazas were the same. If that were the case (and nothing led me to believe it wasn't), Sánchez Mazas was the author of the little diary, which had undoubtedly been written during the days he spent wandering in the forest, or at most very shortly afterwards. To judge by the last text in the notebook, Sánchez Mazas knew the date of the execution had been 30 January 1939; in any case the numeration preceding each entry of the diary corresponded to the days of the month of February of the same year (the Nationalists had indeed taken Gerona on 4 February). From the text of the diary I deduced that, before availing himself of the protection of the Figueras brothers and

49

Angelats, Sánchez Mazas had found a more or less secure refuge in a house in the area, and this house could be none other than the Borrell house or farm, whose inhabitants he thanked and promised a 'substantial monetary reward' and 'an honorary distinction' in the long final declaration, and I also deduced that this house or farm must be in Palol de Rebardit – a municipality bordering on Cornellà de Terri – and that its inhabitants could only be the Ferré family, one of whom was sure to be Maria Ferré, who, as Jaume Figueras had told me at the sudden end of our interview in the Núria, was still alive. All of the above seemed obvious, just as, once fitted together, the place for each piece of a jigsaw puzzle seems obvious. As far as the final declaration went, drawn up in the Mas de la Casa Nova, the place in the forest where the four fugitives had stayed hidden – and undoubtedly when they knew themselves to be safe – it also seemed obvious that it was a way of formalizing Sánchez Mazas' debt to those who'd saved his life, like a safe-conduct enabling them to cross the uncertainties of the immediate post-war period, without having to undergo each and every one of the outrages reserved for the majority of those who, like the Figueras brothers and Angelats, had swelled the ranks of the Republican army. I found it strange, however, that one of the pages torn out of the notebook should be precisely the one containing the declaration in which, it could be inferred, Sánchez Mazas expressed his gratitude to the Figueras brothers and Angelats. I wondered who had torn out that page. And why. I wondered who had torn out the first pages of the notebook, and why. Since every question leads to another, I also wondered – in fact I'd already been wondering this for quite a while – what really happened during those days that Sánchez Mazas wandered aimlessly through the forest in no man's land. What did he think about, what did he feel, what did he tell the Ferrés, the Figueras brothers, Angelats? What did they remember him having told them? And what had they thought and felt? I was yearning to talk to Jaume Figueras' uncle, to Maria Ferré and Angelats, if he were still alive. I told myself, even if Jaume Figueras' tale couldn't be considered trustworthy (or couldn't be considered any more trustworthy than Ferlosio's), for its veracity didn't depend on a memory (his), but on the memory of a memory (his father's) – the accounts of his uncle, Maria Ferré and Angelats (if he was still alive) were on the other hand first-hand reports and therefore, at least at first, much less random than his. I wondered if those tales would fit the reality of events or whether, perhaps inevitably, they'd be varnished with that gloss of half-truth and fibs that always augment an episode now distant and perhaps legendary to its protagonists, so that what they might tell me had happened wouldn't be what really happened or even what they remembered happening, but what they remembered telling before.

Overwhelmed with questions, sure that I'd be lucky if I didn't have to wait more than a month before talking to Figueras' uncle – as if walking over sand dunes and needing to step on terra firma – I called Miquel Aguirre. It was a Monday and it was very late, but Aguirre was still awake and, after telling him about my interview with Jaume Figueras, about the latter's uncle and about Sánchez Mazas' notebook, I asked him if it were possible to obtain documentary proof that Pere Figueras, Jaume's father, had indeed been in prison after the end of the war.

'Couldn't be easier,' he answered. 'In the City Archives there's a register of all the names of every single person who's been imprisoned since before the war. If Pere Figueras was in jail, his name will be there. For sure.'

'Couldn't they have sent him to another prison?'

'Impossible. Everyone detained in the Banyoles area was sent to Gerona prison.'

The next day, before going to work at the newspaper, I presented myself at the City Archives, which were located in a renovated convent, in the old part of the city. Following the signs, I went up a stone stairway and entered the library, a spacious, sunny room, with big windows, gleaming wooden tables bristling with lamps, the silence of which was broken only by the typing of an employee almost completely hidden behind a computer. I told the clerk – a man with unruly hair and a grey moustache – what I was looking for; he stood up, went to a shelf and got down a ring binder.

'Look in here,' he said, handing it to me. 'Beside each name is a file number; if you want to consult one, let me know.'

I sat down at a table and looked through the index, which ran from 1924 to 1949, for a Figueras who'd been held in prison in 1939 or 1940. Since it's quite a common surname in the region, there were several, but none of them were the Pere (or Pedro) Figueras Bahí I was looking for: no one of that name had been in Gerona prison in 1939 or 1940, not even in 1941 or 1942, which was when, according to Jaume Figueras' tale, his father had been in jail. I looked up from the binder: the employee was still typing at his computer; the room was still deserted. Beyond the windows which were flooded with light was a confusion of decrepit houses which,

I thought, wouldn't have looked much different sixty years and a few months before, when, in the final days of the war, a few kilometres away three anonymous lads and an illustrious man in his forties, hid and awaited the end of the nightmare. As if struck by a sudden realization, I thought: 'It's all a lie.' I reasoned that, if the first fact I attempted to confirm independently – Pere Figueras' time in prison – turned out to be false, nothing prevented me from supposing the rest of the tale to be equally untrue. I told myself that there had undoubtedly been three lads who helped Sánchez Mazas survive in the forest after the firing squad – a certainty supported by various circumstances, among them the coincidences between the notes in Sánchez Mazas' notebook and the tale he'd told his son – but certain clues lent credence to the suspicion that it wasn't the Figueras brothers and Angelats. First of all, in Sánchez Mazas' notebook their names had been written in ink and in a different handwriting from the rest of the text, which was in pencil; undoubtedly, then, a hand other than that of Sánchez Mazas had added them. Furthermore, the missing page of the final declaration – where, as far as I could tell from studying the notebook, the Figueras brothers and Angelats should be mentioned, because he'd surely have expressed his gratitude for their help, could well have been torn out *precisely* because it didn't mention them, so that someone would come to the very conclusion that I had reached. And as far as Pere Figueras' false prison sentence goes, it would undoubtedly have been invented by Pere himself, or his son, or by who knows who; in any case, added to the proud refusal to evade captivity by appealing to the favours of a high Francoist dignitary like

Sánchez Mazas, and the letter in which he denounced some unscrupulous person who tried to get money out of Sánchez Mazas by pretending to be him, the story amounted to ideal cement for building one of those legends of paternal heroism which – without anyone ever happening to identify their origins – so prosper at the death of a father in the kind of families inclined to their own mythogenesis. More disappointed than perplexed, I wondered who then were the real forest friends and who had fabricated that fraud and why; more perplexed than disappointed, I said to myself that maybe, as some had suspected from the beginning, Sánchez Mazas hadn't even been in Collell, and perhaps the whole story of the execution and the circumstances surrounding it were nothing but an immense swindle minutely plotted by Sánchez Mazas' imagination – with the voluntary or involuntary collaboration of relatives, friends, acquaintances and strangers – to cleanse his reputation as a coward, to hide some dishonourable episode in his strange wartime adventure and, most of all so that some credulous investigative reporter, avid for novelties, would reconstruct it sixty years later, redeeming him forever before history.

I put the ring binder back in its place on the shelf, and got ready to leave the library, feeling embarrassed and conned, when, as I passed the computer, the clerk asked me if I'd found what I was looking for. I confessed that I hadn't.

'Oh, but don't give up so quickly.' He stood up and, not giving me time to explain anything, went to the shelf and got the binder down again. 'What's the person's name?'

'Pere or Pedro Figueras Bahí. But don't worry: he probably wasn't ever in any prison.'

'Then he won't be here,' he said, but insisted: 'Have you an idea of when he might have been in prison?'

'In '39,' I yielded. 'At the latest '40 or '41.'

The clerk quickly found the page.

'No one of that name,' he confirmed. 'But the prison officer could have made an error in writing it down.' He smoothed his moustache and muttered: 'Let's see . . .'

He flipped ahead and back through the pages of the register several times, running down the lists of names with his index finger, which finally stopped.

'Piqueras Bahí, Pedro,' he read. 'That must be him. Wait a moment, please.'

He went out through a side door and returned a short while later, smiling and carrying a document case with faded covers.

'There's your man,' he said.

The document case did in fact contain Pere Figueras' dossier. Extremely excited, my self-esteem suddenly restored, and telling myself that if Pere Figueras' prison stay wasn't an invention then nor was the rest of the story, I examined the dossier. It stated that Pere Figueras was a native of Sant Andreu del Terri, a municipality assimilated over time into Cornellà de Terri. That he was a farmer and single. That he was twenty-five years old. That his background was un-known. That he'd been incarcerated in the prison of the Military Government, without any charge being laid against him, on 27 April 1939, and that he'd left it not even two months later on 19 June. It also stated that he'd been released by the General Auditor in accordance with an order included in the dossier of a certain Vicente Vila Rubirola. I looked up Rubirola in the index, found him, and asked the clerk for his dossier, which he brought me. A member of the Catalan Republican Left, Rubirola had been in prison after the revolution of 1934 and had been sent back there at the end of the war, the very same day as Pere Figueras and his eight comrades from Cornellà de Terri; all of them were freed on 19 June, the same day as Figueras, in accordance with an order from the Auditor General, which didn't specify any reason justifying this decision; Vila Rubirola, however, had been sent back to jail in June of the same year and having been tried and found guilty, hadn't finally left it again for another twenty years.

I thanked the archive clerk and, as soon as I got to the newspaper office I phoned Aguirre. Many of the names of those imprisoned with Figueras were familiar to him — the majority notorious activists of left-wing parties — and especially Vila Rubirola, who in the early days of the war had participated in the assassination, in Barcelona, of the Secretary-General of the Municipality of Cornellà de Terri. According to Aguirre, the fact that Pere Figueras and his eight comrades were incarcerated without explanation was perfectly normal at the time, when everyone who'd had any kind of military or political link to the Republic had their past submitted to rigorous albeit arbitrary scrutiny, and meanwhile they stayed in prison; nor did he find it strange that Pere Figueras was released after a short time, as this happened often with those the new regime didn't consider a danger.

'What does strike me as odd is that someone as well known as Vila Rubirola, and a few of the others who went into prison with Figueras, should have been released with him,' observed Aguirre. 'And what I really just can't understand is all of them getting out the same day without any explanation, and all so that Vila Rubirola – and I wouldn't be surprised if one or two others – were sent straight back in. I don't get it.' Aguirre fell silent. 'Unless . . .'

'Unless what?'

'Unless someone interceded,' Aguirre concluded, avoiding the name we both had in mind. 'Someone with real power. A hierarch.'

That very evening, having dinner with Conchi in a Greek restaurant, I solemnly announced, because I felt the need to announce it solemnly, that after ten years of not writing a book, the moment had come to try again.

'Bloody brilliant!' shouted Conchi, who was hoping to add a third book to the two escorting her Virgin of Guadalupe in the living room; with a piece of pita bread dipped in tzatziki on its way to her mouth, she added: 'I hope it's not a novel.'

'No,' I said, very confidently. 'It's a true tale.'

'What's that?'

I explained; I think she understood.

'It'll be like a novel,' I summed up. 'Except, instead of being all lies, it's all true.'

'I'm glad it's not going to be a novel.'

'Why's that?'

'No reason,' she answered. 'It's just that – well, honey, I don't think imagination is really your strong suit.'

'You're a real sweetheart, Conchi.'

'Don't take it like that, darling. What I meant to say was . . .' Since she didn't know how to say what she meant to say, she picked up another piece of pita bread and said, 'Anyhow, what's the book about?'

57

'The battle of Salamis.'

'The what?' she screeched.

Several pairs of eyes turned to look at us, for the second time. I knew the story line of my book wasn't going to appeal to Conchi, but, since I didn't want her to kick up a fuss and call everyone's attention to us, I tried to explain it briefly.

'What are you like?' was her comment, accompanied by a look of disgust. 'How can you want to write about a fascist with the number of really good lefty writers there must be around! García Lorca, for example. He was a red, wasn't he? Ooh,' she said not waiting for a reply, reaching under the table: alarmed, I lifted the table cloth up a bit and looked, 'God, my pussy's so itchy.'

'Conchi!' I scolded her in whisper, sitting up quickly and forcing a smile while glancing around at the neighbouring tables, 'I'd appreciate it, when you go out with me, if you'd at least wear panties.'

'What an old fart you are!' she said with her most affectionate smile, but without bringing the submerged hand out into the open; I felt her toes creeping up my calf. 'Don't you think it's sexy? Anyway, when do we start?'

'I've told you a million times I don't like doing it in public toilets.'

'I didn't mean that, dummy. I mean when do we start on the book?'

'Oh that,' I said as one flush went up my leg and another down my face. 'Soon,' I stammered. 'Very soon. As soon as I finish the research.'

But it would actually take me a while yet to reconstruct the story I wanted to tell and to get to know, if not each and every one of its hidden aspects, at least what I judged its essential ones. In fact, for many months I spent all my free time at the newspaper studying the life and work of Sánchez Mazas. I reread his books, I read a lot of the articles he published in the press, many articles by his friends and enemies, his contemporaries, and also everything I came across about the Falange, fascism, the Civil War, and the equivocal, changeable nature of the Franco regime. I scoured libraries, newspaper archives, public records. I travelled to Madrid several times, and constantly to Barcelona, to talk to scholars, professors, friends and acquaintances (or friends of friends and acquaintances of acquaintances) of Sánchez Mazas. I spent an entire morning at the Sanctuary of Collell, which, as I was told by Mossén Juan Prats – the priest with the shiny bald patch and devout smile who showed me the garden with its cypress and palm trees and immense empty halls, low corridors, stairways with wooden handrails and deserted classrooms where Sánchez Mazas and his cellmates had wandered like premonitions of shades – had, once the war was over, gone back to being used as a boarding school for boys until, a year and a half before my visit, it was reduced to its present lonely status of a conference centre for pious associations and occasional lodging for sightseers. It was Father Prats himself, only just born when the events in question occurred in Collell, but not unaware of them, who told me the real or apocryphal story according to which, when Franco's regulars took the Sanctuary, they left not a single prison guard alive. Father Prats also gave me precise directions to get to the spot where the execution took place. Following them, I left the monastery by the access road, arrived at a stone cross commemorating the massacre, turned left down a path which snaked through pines and came out in the clearing. I stayed there for a while, walking beneath the cold sun and immaculate, windy October sky, not doing anything other than sounding out the leafy silence of the forest and trying in vain to imagine the light of another less crystal clear morning, that inconceivable January morning, sixty years ago in the same place, when fifty men suddenly faced death and two of them managed to evade its grasp. As if a revelation by osmosis might await me, I stayed there a while . . . I didn't feel anything. So I left. I went to Cornellà de Terri, because the same day I was having lunch with Jaume Figueras, who that afternoon took me to see Can Borrell, the Ferré's old house, Can Pigem, the Figueras' old house, and the Mas de la Casa Nova, which had been Sánchez Mazas', Angelats' and the Figueras brothers' temporary hiding place. Can Borrell was a farm located in the township of Palol de Rebardit; Can Pigem was in Cornellà de Terri; the Mas de la Casa Nova was between the two villages and in the middle of the woods. Can Borrell was uninhabited, but not in ruins, so was Can Pigem; the Mas de la Casa Nova was uninhabited and in ruins. Sixty years before they'd surely been three quite different houses, but time had virtually equalled them, and their common air of abandonment, of stone skeletons among whose fleshless ribcages the winds groaned in the autumn evening, held not a single suggestion that anyone had ever once lived in them.

It was also thanks to Jaume Figueras, who finally kept his word and acted as diligent intermediary, that I got to speak to his uncle Joachim, Maria Ferré and Daniel Angelats. All three were over eighty: Maria Ferré was eighty-eight; Figueras and

Angelats, eighty-two. All three still had good memories, or at least they still remembered their encounter with Sánchez Mazas and the circumstances surrounding it, as if it had been a determining moment in their lives and they'd often recalled it. Their three versions differed, but weren't contradictory, and at more than one point they were complementary, so from their testimonies, and filling in the gaps they left by means of logic and a little imagination, it wasn't difficult to reconstruct the puzzle of Sánchez Mazas' adventure. Perhaps because no one has time any more to listen to people of a certain age, much less when they start remembering incidents from their youth, all three were anxious to talk, and more than once I had to channel the disorderly flow of their recollections. I can imagine they might have embellished some secondary factors, some lateral details; not that they lied, because among other reasons, if they had, the lie wouldn't have fitted into the puzzle and would have given them away. In all other respects, the three of them were so different that to my eyes the only thing that linked them was their condition as survivors, that deceptive added prestige the protagonists of the bland, routine inglorious present, often concede to the protagonists of the past, which because we only know it through the filter of memory, is always extraordinary, tumultuous, heroic: Figueras was tall and well-built, with an almost youthful air – checked shirt, sailor's cap, well-worn jeans – a travelled man, possessing an enormous vitality and a conversational manner erupting with gestures, exclamations and hearty laughs; Maria Ferré who, according to what Jaume Figueras told me later, had coquettishly visited the hairdresser's before receiving me in her house in Cornellà de Terri – a house that at times had

61

been the village bar and general store, and still at the entrance, almost like relics, stood a marble counter and a set of scales – was slight and sweet, digressive, with eyes that at one moment were mischievous and the next would brim with tears at her inability to dodge the tricks nostalgia set for her in the course of her tale, young eyes, with the colour and fluidity of a summer stream. As for Angelats, my interview with him was crucial. Crucial for me, I mean – or, more precisely, for this book.

For many years, Angelats ran a boarding house in part of a decrepit and beautiful country house in the centre of Banyoles with a large pillared courtyard and immense gloomy lounges. When I met him he'd just survived a heart attack and he was a morose, diminished man, whose gestures, of an almost abbot-like solemnity, contrasted with the childish innocence of many of his observations and the deliberate humility of his Catalan small businessman's demeanour. I don't know if I'm exaggerating here, but I believe that Angelats, like Figueras and Maria Ferré, felt flattered in a way by my interest in him; I know he very much enjoyed remembering Joaquim Figueras – who'd been his best friend for many years and whom he'd not seen for quite some time – and their shared adventure during the war, and while I heard him make an effort to present it as a youthful escapade without the least importance, I guessed it meant all the world to him, perhaps because he felt it had been the only real adventure in his life, or at least the only one he hadn't needed to fear feeling proud of. He spoke to me about it at length; then he told me about his heart attack, how his business was going, his wife, his children, his only grand-daughter. I realized he'd needed to talk to someone about these things for a long time; I realized I was only listening to him in compensation for him having told me his story. Ashamed, I felt sorry for him and, when I felt I'd repaid my debt, I tried to say goodbye, but since it had started to rain Angelats insisted on seeing me to the bus stop.

'Now that I think of it,' he said as we crossed the puddle-strewn plaza under his umbrella. He stopped, and I couldn't help but think that this memory was nothing but a last minute decoy, to make me stay. 'Before he left, Sánchez Mazas told us he was going to write a book about all that, a book with us in it. He was going to call it *Soldiers of Salamis*; strange title, don't you think? He also said he'd send it to us, but he didn't.' Angelats looked at me now: the light from the street-lamp put a yellow reflection on the lenses of his glasses, and for a moment I saw in his bony eye sockets and in the prominence of his forehead and cheeks and in his open jaw the outline of his skull. 'Do you know if he wrote the book?'

A cold shiver ran up my spine. I was about to say yes; I thought just in time: 'If I tell him he wrote it, he'll want to read it and discover my lie.' Feeling I was somehow betraying Angelats, I said brusquely:

'No.'

'No, he didn't write it or you don't know if he wrote it?'

'I don't know if he wrote it,' I lied. 'But I promise I'll find out.'

'Do that.' Angelats started walking again. 'And, if it turns out he did write it, I'd appreciate it if you'd send it to me. It's sure to mention us, as I told you he always said we saved his life. I'd really like to read that book. You understand, don't you?'

'Of course,' I said and, not yet feeling completely rotten, I added: 'But don't worry: as soon as I find it I'll send it to you.'

The next day, as soon as I got to the newspaper I went to the editor's office and negotiated a leave of absence.

'What?' he asked ironically. 'Another novel?'

'No,' I answered smugly. 'A true tale.'

I explained what I meant. I explained what my true tale was about.

'I like it,' he said. 'Have you got a title yet?'

'I think so,' I answered. '*Soldiers of Salamis.*'

Part Two

SOLDIERS OF SALAMIS

ON 27 APRIL 1939, the very day that Pere Figueras and his eight comrades from Cornellà de Terri were sent to prison in Gerona, Rafael Sánchez Mazas had just been named national advisor to the *Falange Española Tradicionalista y de las JONS* and Vice-President of its Leadership Council; a month had not yet passed since the definitive collapse of the Republic, and four more were yet to go by before Sánchez Mazas would become Minister Without Portfolio in the first post-war government. He had always been an unpleasant, arrogant, despotic man, but was neither petty nor vindictive, and so during that period the waiting room to his office teemed with relatives of prisoners eager to gain his intercession on behalf of old acquaintances or friends who the end of the war had left confined in the cells of the defeat. Nothing leads us to believe he did not do what he could for them. Thanks to his insistence, the Caudillo commuted the death sentence hanging over the head of the poet Miguel Hernández to life imprisonment, but not the one which, one November dawn in 1940, led a firing squad to end the life of Julián Zugazagoitia, a good friend of Sánchez Mazas and Minister in Negrín's government. Months before this pointless murder, just back from a trip to Rome as National Delegate of the *Falange Exterior*, his secretary, the journalist Carlos Sentís, brought him up to date on matters pending and read him the list of persons he'd granted an audience for that morning. Suddenly alert, Sánchez Mazas made him repeat a name; then he stood up, strode across his office, opened the door, stopped in the middle of the waiting room and, scouring the frightened faces crowding it, asked: 'Which of you is Joaquín Figueras?'

Paralyzed by terror, a man with a bereft look and travelling clothes tried to answer, but only succeeded in breaking the solid silence following the question with an indecipherable burbling, while reaching a desperate hand, claw-like, into his jacket pocket. Standing in front of him, Sánchez Mazas wanted to know if he were related to the brothers Pedro and Joaquín Figueras. 'I'm their father,' he managed to articulate with a strong Catalan accent and frantic nodding that didn't abate even when Sánchez Mazas crushed him in a relieved embrace. After the effusive greetings, the two men chatted for a few minutes in the office. Joaquim Figueras recounted that his son Pere had spent the last month and a half in prison in Gerona, groundlessly accused, along with other young men of the village, of taking part in the burning of the Cornellà de Terri church at the beginning of the war and of having been involved in the murder of the Municipal Secretary. Sánchez Mazas didn't let him finish; he left his office through a side door and came back a few moments later.

'That's settled,' he proclaimed. 'When you get back to Cornellà you'll find your son at home.'

Figueras left the office in a euphoric state. On his way down the steps he noticed a piercing pain in his hand and realized he still had it thrust inside his jacket pocket, clutching, with all his strength, a piece of paper torn out of a notebook with green covers where Sánchez Mazas had recorded his debt of gratitude to Figueras' sons. And when he arrived in Cornellà days later and dry-eyed embraced his recently freed son, Joaquim Figueras knew he hadn't been wrong to undertake that hallucinatory trip across a devastated country to see a man he didn't know and whom he'd consider till the end of his days one of the most powerful men in Spain.

He was only partly mistaken. Although he'd always considered it an occupation unworthy of gentlemen, Sánchez Mazas had by then spent more than a decade in politics and would take another few years to leave it, but never in his whole life was he to accumulate so much real power in his hands as right then.

He'd been born in Madrid on 18 February, forty-five years earlier. His father, a military doctor originally from Coria, whose uncle had been royal physician to Alfonso XII, died a few months later, and his mother, María Rosario Mazas y Orbegozo, immediately sought the protection of her family in Bilbao. There, in a five-storey house beside the Deusto Bridge, on Henao Street, cajoled by an army of childless uncles, he spent his childhood and adolescence. The Mazas were a clan of *hidalgos* of liberal traditions and literary inclinations, related to Miguel de Unamuno and solidly anchored in the cream of Bilbao society, from which Sánchez Mazas drew inspiration to construct a few characters for his novels, and from whom he inherited an irrepressible propensity to lordly idleness and an obstinate literary vocation. The latter had once similarly tempted his mother, a clever, illustrious woman who poured all her untimely widow's energy into facilitating her son's career as a writer, a career she herself hadn't wanted or been able to pursue.

Sánchez Mazas didn't let her down. It's true he was a mediocre student, who wandered through various upper-class Catholic boarding schools with more shame than glory before ending up at the Central University of Madrid, and finally the Augustinian María Cristina Royal College for Advanced Studies at the monastery in El Escorial, where in 1916 he graduated in Law. It's equally true, however, that he began to show obvious signs of literary talent quite early. At the age of thirteen he wrote poems in the styles of Zorrilla and Marquina; at twenty he imitated Rubén Darío and Unamuno; by twenty-two he was a mature poet; at twenty-eight his poetic work was essentially complete. With typical aristocratic disdain, he barely bothered to publish them, and if we know his work in its entirety (or almost) it's largely owing to the vigilance of his mother, who transcribed his poems by hand in small notebooks bound in black oilcloth, recording beneath each one its place and date of composition. Moreover, Sánchez Mazas is a good poet; a good minor poet, I mean, which is about all a good poet can aspire to. His verses have only one chord – humble and ancient, mono-tonous and a bit sentimental – but Sánchez Mazas plays it masterfully, drawing from it a clean, natural, prosaic music that can only be sung by the bittersweet melancholy of time that flees and in its flight drags down order and the reliable hierarchies of an abolished world that, precisely because it is abolished, is also an invented, impossible world, almost always equivalent to the impossible, invented world of Paradise.

Although he published only one book of poems in his lifetime, it's possible that Sánchez Mazas always considered himself a poet, and perhaps that's what he essentially was; his contemporaries, however, knew him primarily as the author of chronicles, articles and novels, and especially as a politician, which is exactly what he never considered himself and perhaps what he never essentially was. In June of 1916, a year after publishing his first novel, *Brief Memoirs of Tarín*, and having recently graduated in law, Sánchez Mazas returned to Bilbao, then a headstrong, self-satisfied city, dominated by a buoyant bourgeoisie enjoying a period of economic splendour derived from Spain's neutrality during the First World War. That bonanza found its most conspicuous cultural expression in the magazine *Hermes*, which drew together a handful of Catholic writers, admirers of Eugenio d'Ors, Spanish nationalists, devotees of Roman culture and the values of western civilization, whom Ramón de Basterra baptized with the pompous title, 'Roman School of the Pyrenees'. Basterra was one of the more notorious members of that group of writers, the majority of whom would in time go on to swell the ranks of the Falangists; another was Sánchez Mazas. They would meet for discussions at the Lyon d'Or, a café located in the middle of Gran Vía de López de Haro, where Sánchez Mazas dazzled, as a cultivated, circumspect and rather bombastic conversationalist. José María de Areilza, then a boy, whose father took him to the Lyon d'Or for hot chocolate, remembers him as 'a tall and very thin young man, with tortoiseshell spectacles, his eyes both ardent and weary, with a voice which sometimes became strident when emphasizing some point in an argument'. At that time Sánchez Mazas was already writing assiduously in the newspapers *ABC*, *El Sol*, and *El Pueblo Vasco*, and in 1921 Juan de la Cruz, editor of the latter, sent him as a correspondent to cover the war in Morocco, where he began a lasting friendship of drinking sessions and long nocturnal conversations – which would withstand the rancour of living through a war on opposite sides – with another correspondent from Bilbao called Indalecio Prieto.

Sánchez Mazas' stay in Morocco lasted barely a year, because in 1922 Juan Ignacio Luca de Tena sent him to Rome as *ABC*'s correspondent. He was fascinated by Italy. His youthful passion for classical culture, for the Renaissance, and Imperial Rome were forever crystallized by contact with Rome itself. He lived there for seven years. There he married Liliana Ferlosio, an Italian recently emerged from adolescence whom he practically carried off from her home and with whom he would maintain for the rest of his life a chaotic relationship which produced five children. There he matured as a man and as a writer. There he gained a deserved reputation as a columnist by way of some very literary articles, sophisticated in style and confidently executed – sometimes dense with erudition and lyricism, sometimes vehement with political passion – that are perhaps the best of his work. There, too, he was converted to fascism. In fact, it would not be an exaggeration to claim Sánchez Mazas as Spain's first fascist, and quite correct to say he was its most influential theoretician. Fervent reader of Maurras and intimate friend of Luigi Federzoni – who incarnated in Italy a kind of enlightened, bourgeois fascism, and in the fullness of time would come to hold various ministerial posts in Mussolini's governments – monarchical and conservative by vocation, Sánchez Mazas thought he'd discovered in fascism the ideal instrument to cure his nostalgia for an imperial Catholicism and, especially, to forcibly mend the reliable hierarchies of the *ancien régime* that the old democratic egalitarianism and the vigorous, new Bolshevik egalitarianism were threatening to annihilate all over Europe. Or to put it another way: perhaps for Sánchez Mazas fascism was simply a way of *realizing* his poetry, of making real the world it melancholically evoked – the abolished, invented, impossible world of Paradise. Be that as it may, the fact is he greeted the March on Rome enthusiastically in a series of articles entitled *Italy's Genteel Transition*, and saw Benito Mussolini as the reincarnation of the Renaissance *condottiere* and his ascension to power as the proclamation that the time of heroes and poets had returned to Italy.

So in 1929, back in Madrid, Sánchez Mazas had already made the decision to dedicate himself entirely to ensuring that such a time would also return to Spain. Up to a point he succeeded. War is the time of heroes and poets *par excellence*, and in the thirties few people pledged as much intelligence, as much effort and as much talent as he did to making war break out in Spain. Upon his return to the country, Sánchez Mazas understood straightaway that to achieve his goal it was not only necessary to found a party cut from the same cloth as the one he'd watched triumph in Italy, but also to find a Renaissance *condottiere*, a figure who, when the time came, would symbolically catalyze all the forces liberated by the panic the decomposition of the monarchy and the inevitable triumph of the Republic would generate among the most traditional sectors of Spanish society. The first venture took a while yet to come off; but not the second, for José Antonio Primo de Rivera immediately came to embody the figure of providential *caudillo* Sánchez Mazas was looking for. The friendship that united them was solid and durable (so much so that one of the last letters José Antonio wrote from Alicante prison on the eve of his execution on 20 November 1936 was to Sánchez Mazas); perhaps this was because it was based on an equitable division of roles. José Antonio in fact possessed all that Sánchez Mazas lacked: youth, beauty, physical courage, money and lineage; the opposite was also true: armed with his Italian experience, his extensive reading and literary talent, Sánchez Mazas became José Antonio's most trusted advisor and, once the Falange was founded, its principal ideologue and propagandist and one of the fundamental forgers of its rhetoric and symbols. Sánchez Mazas proposed the party symbol of yoke and arrows, which had been the symbol of the Catholic Monarchs, coined the ritual slogan, 'Arise Spain!', composed the very famous *Prayer for the Falangist Dead*, and over the course of several December nights in 1935 participated, along with José Antonio and other writers of his circle – Jacinto Miquelarena, Agustín de Foxá, Pedro Mourlane Michelena, José María Alfaro y Dionisio Ridruejo – in the writing of the lyrics to the anthem *Face to the Sun*, on the ground floor of Or Kompon, a Basque bar located on Miguel Moya Street in Madrid.

But it would still take some time before Sánchez Mazas was to become the Falange's principal purveyor of rhetoric, as Ramiro Ledesma Ramos called him. When he arrived in Madrid in 1929, surrounded by an aura of prestige as a cosmopolitan writer with brand new ideas, no one in Spain was thinking seriously of founding a party in the fascist mould, not even Ledesma, who a couple of years later would found the JONS, the first Spanish fascist faction. Like life in general, however, literary life was becoming more radical by the minute, heated by the convulsions shaking Europe and the changes that could be glimpsed on the horizon of Spanish politics: in 1927 a young writer called César Arconada, who had subscribed to the elitism of Ortega y Gasset and before long would be swelling the ranks of the Communist Party, summed up the feelings of many people of his age when he declared that 'a young man can be a Communist, a fascist, anything at all, anything as long as he doesn't cling to old liberal ideas'. That explained, in part, why so many writers of the moment, in Spain and all over Europe, changed in so few years from the playful, sporty aestheticism of the roaring twenties to the pure, hard political combat of the ferocious thirties.

Sánchez Mazas was no exception. In fact, the entirety of his pre-war literary activity consists of innumerable articles of hardened prose, where the moral and aesthetic definition of the Falangists — made up of deliberate ideological confusion, mystical exaltation of violence and militarism, and essentialist vulgarities proclaiming the eternal character of the fatherland and the Catholic religion — coexists with a central proposition which, as Andrés Trapiello points out, was basically limited to stocking up on quotes from Latin historians, German thinkers and French poets that would serve to justify the approaching fratricidal assault. Sánchez Mazas' political activity, on the other hand, was frenetic during these years. In February 1933, having taken part in various attempts to create a fascist party, along with the journalist Manuel Delgado Barreto, José Antonio Primo de Rivera, Ramiro Ledesma Ramos, Juan Aparicio and Ernesto Giménez Caballero — with whom for years he carried on a not always buried struggle for the ideological leadership of Spanish fascism, which he eventually won — Sánchez Mazas founded the weekly *El fascio*, which amounted to the first encounter of the various national-syndicalist tendencies which would eventually come together in the Falange. The first and only issue of *El fascio* appeared a month later and was immediately banned by the authorities, but on 29 October of that year the founding act of the Spanish Falange took place in the Madrid Drama Theatre, and Sánchez Mazas, who months later would be assigned party membership card number four (Ledesma had number one; José Antonio two; Ruiz de Alda three; Giménez Caballero five), was named to its Executive Council. From that moment and until 18 July 1936 his influence in the party – a party that before the war never managed to attract more than a hundred members in the entire country, and that never reaped more than a few thousand votes in all the elections for which it stood, but that would be decisive for the future history of the country – was fundamental. During those obdurate years Sánchez Mazas gave speeches, spoke at meetings, designed strategies and programmes, wrote reports, made up slogans, advised his leader and, especially by way of *F.E.*, the official weekly publication of the Falange – where he was in charge of a section called 'Watchwords and Standards of Style' – disseminated, in anonymous articles and others signed by him or by José Antonio himself, ideas and a way of life which, in time and as no one could have suspected – least of all Sánchez Mazas – would eventually become the way of life and ideas, adopted as a revolutionary shock ideology in the face of the urgencies of the war, later lowered to the status of ideological ornament by the chubby, blustering, effeminate, incompetent, astute and conservative soldier who usurped them, finally becoming the increasingly rotten and meaningless paraphernalia with which a handful of boors struggled for forty gloomy years to justify their shitty regime.

However, during the time the war was incubating, the watchwords Sánchez Mazas disseminated still possessed a gleaming suggestion of modernity, that young patriots from good families and the violent ideals they cherished contributed to strengthening. At that time José Antonio was very fond of quoting a phrase of Oswald Spengler's; that at the eleventh hour it had always been a squad of soldiers that had saved civilization. At that time the young Falangists felt they were that squad of soldiers. They knew (or believed they knew) that their families slept an innocent sleep of bourgeois beatitude, not knowing that a wave of impunity and egalitarian barbarism was going to wake them suddenly with a tremendous clamour of catastrophe. They felt their duty was to preserve civilization by force and avoid the catastrophe. They knew (or believed they knew) that they were few, but this mere statistical circumstance did not daunt them. They felt they were heroes. Although he was no longer young and lacked the physical strength, courage and even the essential conviction to be one – but not a family whose innocent sleep of bourgeois beatitude he wished to preserve – Sánchez Mazas also felt it, and thus abandoned literature to give himself over to the cause with priestly devotion. That didn't keep him from frequenting the most exclusive salons of the capital with José Antonio, or from joining him in some of his notorious, seigneurial escapades, like the Charlemagne Dinner Parties, extravagantly sumptuous banquets held in the Hotel París to commemorate the Emperor; but especially to protest with their rigorous aristocratic exquisiteness against the democratic and republican vulgarity lying in wait on the other side of the hotel's walls. The most assiduous meetings of José Antonio and his constant entourage of poet soldiers took place downstairs at the Café Lyon, on Alcalá Street, in a place known as La Ballena Alegre, where they would argue heatedly, until the small hours, about politics and literature, and where they coexisted in an atmosphere of false cordiality with young left-wing writers with whom they shared anxieties and beer, conversations, jokes and polite insults.

The outbreak of war was to change this deceptive, affectionate hostility into real hostility, though the unstoppable deterioration of political life during the thirties had already announced the imminence of the change to whomever wanted to see it. Those who months, weeks or even days earlier had talked over a cup of coffee, on the way out of a theatre or at an exhibition of works by a mutual friend, now found themselves embroiled on opposite sides in street fights which disdained neither the crack of gunfire nor the shedding of blood. The violence, in reality, had been around for a while and, despite the protests of victimization by some party leaders, opposed to it temperamentally and by education, the fact is that the Falange had been systematically feeding it, with the aim of making the Republic's situation untenable; the use of force was at the very heart of the Falangist ideology, which, like all the other fascist movements, adopted Lenin's revolutionary methods, for whom a minority of brave and committed men – the equivalent of Spengler's squad of soldiers – was enough to take power through armed struggle. Like José Antonio, Sánchez Mazas was also one of those Falangists who was sometimes, in theory, reluctant to use violence (in practice he encouraged it:

having read Georges Sorel, who considered it a moral imperative, his own writings are almost always an incitement) that's why in February 1934, in the *Prayer for the Falangist Dead*, composed at the request of José Antonio to put a stop to his men's desire for revenge after the murder of the student Matías Montero in a street brawl, he wrote: 'To a victory that's not clear, gentlemanly and generous, we prefer defeat, because while every blow our enemies deal is horrendous and cowardly, each of our actions must be the affirmation of a higher valour and morality.' Time proved these lovely words to be nothing but rhetoric. At a meeting held at the Parador de Gredos on 16 June 1935, the leadership of the Falange, convinced it would never reach power by way of elections and that its very existence as a political party was in danger – for the Republic rightly considered it a permanent threat to its survival – took the decision to embark on the conquest of power through armed insurrection. During the year following that meeting, the conspiratorial manoeuvrings of the Falange – replete as they were with innumerable suspicions, hesitations, provisos, and doubts that conveyed both their scant confidence in their own possibilities of triumph and their leader's prescient fears that the party and its revolutionary programme would be devoured by the predictable alliance of the army with the most conservative sectors of society who would support the coup – did not cease for an instant, until on 14 March 1936, after being decimated in the elections of February that year, the Falange was beheaded when the police closed its premises on Nicasio Gallego Street, arrested its entire Leadership Council and banned the party *sine die*.

*   *   *

After that Sánchez Mazas' trail vanishes. One can only attempt to reconstruct his adventures during the months before the conflict and during the three years it lasted by way of partial testimonies – fleeting allusions in memoirs and documents of the time, tales told by those who shared snippets of his adventures, memories of relatives and friends to whom he'd recounted his memories – and also through the veil of a legend shimmering with errors, contradictions and ambiguities which Sánchez Mazas' selective loquacity about this turbulent period of his life did nothing but nourish. So then, what follows is not what actually happened, but rather what seems probable might have happened; I'm not offering proven facts, but reasonable conjectures.

Here they are:

In March of 1936, when Sánchez Mazas is being held in the Modelo Prison in Madrid along with his Falange leadership comrades, his fourth child, Máximo, is born, and Victoria Kent, at that time General Director of Prisons, grants the inmate the three days' leave to visit his wife, which he's entitled to by law, on condition that he give his word of honour not to leave Madrid and to return to the prison at the end of the allotted time. Sánchez Mazas accepts the deal, but, according to another of his sons, Rafael, before he leaves the jail the governor summons him to his office and tells him, off the record, that he sees things getting very dark, half suggesting 'that he would be better off not coming back, and that he, for his part, wouldn't go too far out of his way to find and recapture him'. Since this justifies Sánchez Mazas' later dubious behaviour, the truth of this version could well be called into question; yet equally, one could imagine it not being false. The fact is that Sánchez Mazas, forgetting the protests of gentlemanly behaviour and heroism with which he illustrated so many pages of incendiary prose, breaks his word and flees to Portugal, but José Antonio – who had taken his deputy's words seriously and who judged that not only was his honour at stake, but that of the entire Falange – orders him from his prison cell in Alicante, where he'd been transferred along with his brother Miguel on the night of 5 June, to return to Madrid. Sánchez Mazas obeys, but before he can turn himself back over to the Modelo Prison the uprising breaks out.

The following days are confusing. Almost three years later, Eugenio Montes – whom Sánchez Mazas called 'my grandest and greatest comrade in the drive to put human words at the service of our Falange' – describes from Burgos his friend's situation in the days immediately after 18 July as 'an adventure of street corners and hideouts, with the red henchmen hot on his heels'. The phrase is as novelistic as it is elusive, but perhaps doesn't entirely betray the truth. Revolution triumphs in Madrid. People kill and die in back alleys and barracks. The legitimate government has lost control of the situation and the atmosphere is thick with a lethal mixture of fear and euphoria. Houses are searched; militiamen's control spreads through the streets. One night at the beginning of September, unable to stand the anxiety of secrecy and the constant imminence of danger any longer, or perhaps urged by his friends or acquaintances who'd been running the risk of giving cover to a fugitive of his importance for too long, Sánchez Mazas decides to leave his lair, flee Madrid and cross over into the Nationalist zone.

Predictably, he doesn't make it. The next day, as soon as he leaves the house, he gets stopped; the patrol demands he identify himself. With a strange mixture of panic and resignation, Sánchez Mazas realizes he is lost and, as if wanting to take his leave of reality in silence, for a second of indecision that seems interminable he looks around and sees that, though it's only nine o'clock, the shops on Montera Street have already opened and the urgent, everyday hustle and bustle of the crowd floods the pavements, while the harsh sun foretells another suffocating morning of this never-ending summer. At that moment the attention of the three armed militiamen is caught by a truck stuffed with members of the General Workers' Union bristling with weapons and war cries, heading for the front at Guadarrama with the bodywork painted with initials and names, among them that of Indalecio Prieto, who's just been named Minister of the Airforce and Navy in Largo Caballero's incendiary government. Then Sánchez Mazas thinks up a desperate idea and acts on it: he tells the militiamen that he cannot identify himself because he's undercover in Madrid carrying out a mission entrusted to him directly by the Minister of the Airforce and Navy, and demands they put him in contact with Prieto immediately. Caught between bewilderment and suspicion, the militiamen decide to take him to the headquarters of the State Security Office to check the authenticity of his implausible excuse; there, after a few anguished attempts, Sánchez Mazas manages to speak to Prieto by telephone. Concerned about the situation, Prieto advises him to seek refuge in the Chilean Embassy and affectionately wishes him good luck; then, in the name of their old friendship in Africa, orders his immediate release.

That same day Sánchez Mazas manages to get into the Chilean Embassy, where he will spend almost a year and a half. There is a photograph from this spell of confinement: Sánchez Mazas appears in the centre of a chorus of refugees, among whom is the Falangist writer Samuel Ros; there are eight of them, all a little ragged and unshaven, all expectant. Wearing an undershirt that was perhaps once white, with his Semitic profile, his spectacles and broad forehead, Sánchez Mazas is leaning elegantly on a desk on which there is nothing but an empty glass, a piece of bread, a sheaf of papers or notebooks and a hungry saucepan. He is reading; the rest listen to him. What he reads is an excerpt from *Rosa Krüger*, a novel he wrote or began to write in those days to relieve the tedium of confinement and distract his companions, and which would only be published, unfinished, fifty years later, when its author had already been dead for a long time. It is, without doubt, his best novel and also a good novel, as well as being strange and rather atemporal, written in a Byzantine style by someone with the taste and sensibility of a Pre-Raphaelite painter, with a Europeanist vocation and a patriotic, conservative background, saturated with exquisite fantasies, exotic adventures, and a kind of melancholic sensuality across which, in a crystalline and exact prose, it recounts the battle waged in the mind of the protagonist between the two essential principles, which according to the author govern the universe – the diabolical and the angelic – and the final victory of the latter, incarnated in a *donna angelicata* called Rosa Krüger. It's surprising that Sánchez Mazas managed to isolate himself from the obligatory and noisy promiscuity that reigned in the Embassy in order to write his book – but not that the fruit of this isolation should so meticulously evade the dramatic circumstances surrounding its conception, for it would have been pointless to add to the tragedy of the war the tale of the tragedy of the war. Furthermore, the apparent contradiction, which has so preoccupied some of his readers, between Sánchez Mazas' bellicose Falangist ideas and his apolitical and aestheticizing literary task, is resolved if we admit that both are conflicting but coherent expressions of one nostalgia: for the abolished, impossible and invented world of Paradise, for the safe hierarchies of an *ancien régime* which the inevitable winds of history were sweeping away forever.

As time passes and the bloodletting and desperation of the war increases, the situation in the embassies harbouring refugees in Republican Madrid gets more and more precarious, and the fear of attacks intensifies, so that anyone who has a reasonable possibility of escape prefers to run the risk of the adventure in search of a safe refuge rather than prolong the anxious uncertainty of confinement and waiting. That's what Samuel Ros does, arriving in Chile in the middle of 1937, not to return to Nationalist Spain until the following year. Encouraged by Ros's success, at some point in the autumn of 1937 Sánchez Mazas attempts to escape. He has the help of a prostitute and a young Falangist sympathizer whose family has or had a transport company, and who are acquaintances of Sánchez Mazas. His plan is to get to Barcelona and, once there, engage the help of the fifth column to make contact with the escape networks that smuggled people across the French border. They put the plan into action and, for several days, Sánchez Mazas travels by secondary roads and cart tracks, camouflaged under a load of rotting vegetables, the 600 kilometres between him and Barcelona in the company of the prostitute and the young Falangist. Miraculously, they make it past all the control posts and arrive safe and sound at their destination, with no setbacks more serious than a blown-out tyre and getting the fright of their lives from a dog with an overly sensitive nose. The three travellers separate in Barcelona, and Sánchez Mazas is received, just as planned, by a lawyer who belongs to the JMB, one of the numerous, unconnected Falangist factions the fifth column have scattered throughout the city. After granting him a few days rest, the members of the JMB urge him to take command and, asserting his right as member number four of the Falange, assemble all the fifth columnist splinter groups and submit them to party discipline, obliging them to coordinate their activities. Perhaps because his only preoccupation up to that moment has been to get out of the red zone and cross over into Nationalist territory, or simply because he knows himself incapable of action, the offer surprises him, and he refuses outright on the grounds of his complete ignorance of the situation in the city and the groups operating within it; but the members of the JMB, who are as young and bold as they are inexperienced, and who greeted his arrival as a gift from providence, insist, and he has no choice but to accept.

Over the following days Sánchez Mazas meets with representatives of other fifth-column factions and one morning, on his way to the Iberia, a bar in the city centre where the owner is a sympathizer of the Nationalist cause, he is arrested by military intelligence agents. This is 29 November 1937; versions of what happens next differ. There are those who maintain that Father Isidoro Martín, who had been Sánchez Mazas' professor at the María Cristina Royal College at El Escorial, intercedes in vain on his behalf, to Manuel Azaña, who had also been a student of his at that school. Julián de Zugazagoitia, whom at the end of the war Sánchez Mazas unsuccessfully tried to save from the firing squad, affirms that he proposed to President Negrín that they exchange him for the journalist Federico Angulo, and that Azaña hinted at the expediency of swapping the writer for some compromising manuscripts of his own that were in seditious hands. Another version maintains that Sánchez Mazas didn't even make it as far as Barcelona, because after leaving the Chilean Embassy he sought refuge in the Polish one, which was attacked, and that was when Azorín intervened to spare him a death sentence. There are even those who claim Sánchez Mazas actually was swapped at some point during the war. These last two hypotheses are erroneous; almost certainly the first two are not. However it happened, the truth is that, after being arrested by the SIM, Sánchez Mazas was sent to the *Uruguay*, a ship anchored in the port of Barcelona and converted into a floating prison earlier in the war, and later taken to the Palace of Justice, where he was tried along with other fifth columnists. During the trial he was accused of being the Commander-in-Chief of the fifth column in Barcelona, which was false, and of incitement to rebellion, which was true. However, unlike most of the rest of the accused, Sánchez Mazas was not condemned to death. This is puzzling; perhaps only another intervention from afar by Indalecio Prieto can explain it.

Once the trial is over, Sánchez Mazas is returned to the *Uruguay*, and passes the following months in one of its cells. The living conditions are not good: food is scarce; the treatment brutal. News of the war is also scarce, but as it progresses, even the prisoners on the *Uruguay* understand that

Franco's victory is near. On 24 January 1939, two days before Yagüe's troops enter Barcelona, he's awakened by an unusual sound, and before long notices the jailers' nervousness. For a moment he thinks they're going to release him; then he thinks they're going to shoot him. He spends the morning lurching between these two agonizing alternatives. At about three in the afternoon a SIM agent orders him out of his cell, off the boat and onto a bus parked on the dock, where another fourteen prisoners from the *Uruguay* and the Vallmajor *checa* are waiting, along with the sixteen SIM agents in charge of their custody. Among the prisoners are two women, Sabina González de Carranceja and Juana Aparicio Pérez del Pulgar; also among them is José María Poblador, an early leader of the JONS and important player in the putsch of July 1936, and Jesús Pascual Aguilar, one of the leaders of the Barcelona fifth column. What no one can know at this moment is that of all the male prisoners making up the convoy, by the end of the week only Sánchez Mazas, Pascual and Poblador will still be alive.

Silently the bus crosses Barcelona, which has been changed by the terror of exodus and the wintry sky into a ghostly desolation of boarded-up windows and balconies, and wide ashen avenues with the disorderly air of an abandoned refugee camp, and traversed only, if at all, by furtive transients who gnash their teeth like wolves looking hungry and ready to flee as they pass craters in the pavement, protected from adversity and from the glacial wind only by threadbare overcoats. Upon leaving Barcelona by the road to exile, the spectacle turns apocalyptic: an avalanche of men and women, old people and children, soldiers and civilians together, carrying clothing, mattresses and household goods, advancing laboriously with the unmistakable trudge of the defeated or riding on carts or mules of despair, the road and ditches overflowing with people strewn intermittently with corpses of animals with their guts exposed or abandoned vehicles. The caravan crawls forward interminably. Sometimes it stops; sometimes, with a mixture of disbelief, hatred and immeasurable weariness, someone stares hard at the occupants of the bus, envying their comfort and shelter, ignorant of their firing squad fate; every now and then someone hurls an insult. Sometimes, as well, a Nationalist airplane flies over the road and spits out a few bursts of machine-gun fire or drops a bomb, provoking a panicked stampede among the refugees and a faint hope among the prisoners on the bus, who at some point even cherish the illusion – soon belied by the strict watch the SIM agents keep over them – that they could take advantage of the chaos of an attack to escape across the countryside.

The night is black by the time they make their way through Gerona and later Banyoles. Then they turn off on a dirt road that snakes its way through shadowy woods and eventually stop before a stretch of stone wall dotted with lights, like a colossal galleon capsized in the middle of the darkness, which is polluted by the jailers' barked orders. It is the Sanctuary of Santa María del Collell. Sánchez Mazas will spend five days there together with the other two thousand prisoners from what remains of Republican Spain, including several deserters from the reds and several members of the International Brigades. Before the war the monastery had been a boarding school where the brothers taught secondary students in classrooms with enormously high ceilings and gigantic windows overlooking earth-floored courtyards and gardens lined with cypresses, where there were long, low corridors and vertiginous staircases with wooden handrails; now the boarding school has been converted into a prison, the classrooms into cells, and in the patios, corridors and staircases the adolescent hubbub of the boarders no longer echoes, instead just the hopeless footsteps of the incarcerated. The prison governor is a man called Monroy, the same one who ruled the prison-ship *Uruguay* with an iron hand; however, at Collell the prison regime is less strict: it is not forbidden to speak to those who serve the food nor with those met in the coming and going from the lavatories; the food is still foul and scant, but sometimes a furtive cigarette appears in a cell, and is eagerly shared round. The cell Sánchez Mazas occupies is on the top floor of the old boarding school, and it's bright and spacious; along with him and several International Brigadistas who speak no intelligible language, it is occupied by the doctor Fernando de Marimón, the naval captain Gabriel Martín Morito, Father Guiu, Jesús Pascual and José María Poblador, who can hardly walk because his legs are covered in boils. On the second day the Brigadistas are released and their places taken by Nationalist prisoners captured at Teruel and Belchite; the cell fills up. Sometimes they let them go out and walk around the courtyard or in the gardens; they are not guarded by SIM agents or Carabineros (although the monastery swarms with both): they are guarded by soldiers as malnourished and ragged as themselves, who make jokes or hum popular songs between their teeth as they kick the garden stones in boredom or watch them indifferently. The hours of confinement and inactivity foster intrigue: given the nearness of the border, and especially from the moment a big shot like

Sánchez Mazas joined the string of prisoners, many cherish the hope of being exchanged before long, a hypothesis that weakens as time goes on. The hours they share also give rise to the consolation of friendship. As if magically foreseeing that he'd be one of the survivors of the confinement, and the only one who, years later, will tell the horror of those final hours in a meticulous and Manichean book, Sánchez Mazas became especially friendly with Pascual, who only knew of him from reading his articles in *F.E.*, and to whom Sánchez Mazas recounted his odyssey through the war: he tells him about the Modelo prison, about the birth of his son Máximo, about the uncertain days following the uprising, about Indalecio Prieto and the Chilean Embassy, about Samuel Ros and *Rosa Krüger*, about his clandestine trip across enemy Spain in a delivery truck in the company of a rich kid and a prostitute, about Barcelona and the JMB and the fifth column and his trial and finally about the prison-ship *Uruguay*.

At dusk on the 29th, Sánchez Mazas, Pascual and his cellmates are taken to the roof of the monastery, a place they've never been before and where they are assembled with other prisoners, 500 in total, maybe more. Pascual knows some of them – Pedro Bosch Labrús, Viscount Bosch Labrús and airforce captain Emilio Leucona – but barely manages to exchange a few words with them before a Carabinero immediately orders silence and begins to read out a list of names. Because the hope of a prisoner swap comes to mind again, as soon as he hears the name of someone he knows Pascual desires heart and soul to be included in the list, but, without any precise reason for this shift in opinion, by the time the Carabinero pronounces his name – shortly after that of

90

Sánchez Mazas and immediately following Bosch Labrús – he has already regretted formulating this wish. The twenty-five men who have been named, among whom are all of Sánchez Mazas and Pascual's cellmates except Fernando de Marimón, are taken to a cell on the first floor where there are only a few desks pushed against the crumbling walls and a blackboard with patriotic historical dates scribbled in chalk. The door closes behind them and an ominous silence falls, soon broken by someone declaring that they are about to be exchanged and who manages to distract the anguish of a few of them with the discussion of a conjecture that fades away after a while to make room for unanimous pessimism. Sitting at a desk at one end of the cell, before the evening meal Father Guiu hears the confession of some of the prisoners, and then prepares communion. No one sleeps that night: lit by a grey stoney light that comes in through the window, giving their faces a hint of their future cadaverous appearance (although as time passes the grey thickens and the darkness becomes real), the prisoners stay awake listening through the wall to noises in the corridor or seeking illusory comfort in memories or in a last conversation. Sánchez Mazas and Pascual are stretched out on the floor, leaning their backs against the cold wall, their legs covered by one insufficient blanket; neither of them will remember exactly what they talked about during that scant night, but both will recall the long silences punctuating their secret meeting, the whispers of their companions and the sound of their sleepless coughing, the rain falling, indifferent, assiduous, black and freezing on the paving stones in the courtyard and the cypresses in the garden; and it keeps falling until dawn of 30 January slowly changes the darkness of the windows for the sickly whitish, ghostly colour that stains the atmosphere in the cell like a premonition at the moment the jailer orders them out.

No one has slept, everyone seems to have been awaiting that moment and, as if drawn by the urgency of resolving the uncertainty, they obey with somnambulant diligence and gather in the courtyard with another similar-sized group of prisoners, to bring the number to fifty. They wait a few minutes, docile, silent and soaked, under a fine rain and a sky thick with clouds, and finally a young man appears in whose indistinct features Sánchez Mazas recognizes the indistinct features of the warden of the *Uruguay*. He tells them they are going to be put to work at an aviation camp under construction in Banyoles and orders them to form into ten lines, five deep; while obeying, unthinkingly taking the first place on the right in the second line, Sánchez Mazas feels his heart bolt: in the grip of panic, he realizes the aviation camp can only be an excuse – senseless to build one with the Nationalist troops launching a definitive offensive a few kilometres away. He begins to walk at the head of the group, unhinged and shaking, unable to think clearly, absurdly searching the blank faces of the armed soldiers lining the road for a sign or a glimmer of hope, trying in vain to convince himself that at the end of that journey what awaited him was something other than death. Beside him, or behind him, someone is trying to justify or explain something he doesn't hear or doesn't understand, because every step he takes absorbs all his attention, as if it might be his last; beside him or behind him, the sickly legs of José María Poblador say, Enough, and the prisoner collapses in a puddle and is helped up and dragged back to the monastery by two soldiers. A hundred and fifty metres on from this, the group turns left, leaves the road and goes up into the forest along a path of chalky soil that opens out into a clearing: a wide expanse surrounded by pine trees. From out of the woods booms a military voice ordering them to halt and face left. Terror seizes the group, which stops in its tracks; almost all its members automatically turn to the left, but dread confuses the instinct of others who, like Captain Gabriel Martín Morito, turn to the right. For an instant, which feels eternal, Sánchez Mazas thinks he's going to die. He thinks the bullets that are going to kill him will come from behind his back, which is where the commanding voice had come from, and that, before he dies from bullets hitting him, they'll have to hit the four men lined up behind him. He thinks he's not going to die, that he's going to escape. He thinks that he can't escape to the back because the shots will come from there; nor to his left, because he'd run back out to the road and the soldiers; nor ahead, because he'd have to jump over a wall of eight utterly terrified men. But (he thinks) he can escape towards the right, where no more than six or seven metres away a dense thicket of pines and undergrowth holds a promise of hiding. To the right, he thinks. And he thinks: Now or never. At that moment several machine guns stationed behind the group, exactly where the commander's voice had come from, begin to sweep the clearing; trying to protect themselves, the prisoners instinctively seek the ground. By then Sánchez Mazas has reached the thicket, he runs between pines that scratch his face with the pitiless clatter of the machine guns still ringing in his ears, finally trips providentially and is flung, rolling over mud and wet leaves, into the ravine at the edge of the plateau, landing in a swampy ditch at the mouth of a stream. Because he rightly imagines that his pursuers imagine him trying to get as far away from them as possible, he decides to shelter there, relatively close to the clearing – cringing, panting, soaking wet and with his heart pounding in his throat, covering himself as best he can with leaves and mud and pine boughs, hearing his unfortunate companions receiving *coups de grâce* – and then the barking of the dogs and the shouts of the Carabineros urging the soldiers to find the fugitive or fugitives (because Sánchez Mazas doesn't yet know that, infected by his irrational impulse to abscond, Pascual has also managed to escape the massacre). For a length of time he has no idea whether to measure in minutes or hours, while he scratches ceaselessly at the ground to cover himself in mud till his fingernails are bleeding and hopes that the incessant rain will prevent the dogs from finding his trail, Sánchez Mazas keeps hearing shouts and barks and shots, until at some moment he senses something shift behind him and urgently turns around, cringing like a cornered rat.

Then he sees him. He's standing beside the ditch, tall and burly and silhouetted against the dark green of the pines and the dark blue of the clouds, panting a little, his large hands grasping the slanted rifle and the field uniform with all its buckles, threadbare from exposure. Prey to the aberrant resignation of one who knows his time has come, through his thick glasses blurred by the rain, Sánchez Mazas looks at the soldier who is going to kill him or hand him over – a young man, his hair plastered to his skull by the rain, his eyes maybe grey, his cheeks gaunt and cheekbones prominent – and remembers him or thinks he remembers him from among the ragged soldiers who guarded them in the monastery. He recognizes him or thinks he recognizes him, but takes no comfort from the idea that it's going to be him and not a SIM agent who redeems him from the endless agony of fear, and it humiliates him like an injury added to all the injuries of these years on the run not to have died with his cellmates or not to have known how to die in an open field in broad daylight and fighting with a courage he lacked, instead of dying now and there, muddy and alone and shaking with dread and shame in an undignified hole in the ground. So, his mind raving and confused, Rafael Sánchez Mazas — exquisite poet, fascist ideologue, Franco's future minister — awaits the shot that will finish him off. But the shot doesn't come, and Sánchez Mazas, as if he were already dead and from death remembering this scene from a dream, watches guilelessly as the soldier slowly advances towards the edge of the ditch in the unceasing rain and the threatening sound of soldiers and Carabineros, just steps away, the rifle pointing at him unostentatiously, the gesture more inquisitive than tense, like a novice hunter about to identify his first prey, and just as the soldier gets to the edge of the ditch the vegetal noise of the rain is pierced by a nearby shout:

'Is anyone there?'

The soldier is looking at him; Sánchez Mazas is looking at the soldier, but his weak eyes don't understand what they see: beneath the sodden hair and wide forehead and eyebrows covered in raindrops the soldier's look doesn't express compassion or hatred, or even disdain, but a kind of secret or unfathomable joy, something verging on cruelty, something that resists reason, but nor is it instinct, something that remains there with the same blind stubbornness with which blood persists in its course and the earth in its immovable orbit and all beings in their obstinate condition of being, something that eludes words the way the water in the stream eludes stone, because words are only made for saying to each other, for saying the sayable, when the sayable is everything except what rules us or makes us live or matters or what we are or what this anonymous defeated soldier is, who now looks at this man whose body almost blends in with the earth and the brown water in the ditch, and who calls out loudly without taking his eyes off him:

'There's nobody over here!'

Then he turns and walks away.

For nine days and nights of the brutal winter of 1939 Rafael Sánchez Mazas wandered through the region of Banyoles trying to cross the lines of the Republican army in retreat and pass over into the Nationalist zone. Many times he thought he wasn't going to make it; alone, no other resources than his will to survive, unable to get his bearings in unfamiliar territory of wild, dense woods, weakened to the point of exhaustion from walking, by the cold, hunger and three uninterrupted years of captivity, many times he had to stop to gather his strength in order not to let himself just give up. The first three days were terrible. He slept during the day and walked at night, avoiding the exposure of the roads and villages, begging for food and shelter at farms, and though he prudently dared not reveal his true identity at any of them, but rather introduced himself as a lost Republican soldier, and though almost everyone he asked gave him something to eat, let him rest awhile and gave him directions without asking questions, fear kept anyone from offering him protection. At dawn on the fourth day, after more than three hours wandering through dark forests, Sánchez Mazas made out a farm in the distance. Less by rational decision than out of utter fatigue, he collapsed onto a bed of pine needles and remained there, his eyes closed, barely sensing the sound of his own breathing and the smell of the dew-soaked earth. He had eaten nothing since the morning before, he was exhausted and felt ill, because not a single muscle in his body didn't ache. Until then the miracle of having survived the firing squad and the hope of encountering the Nationalists had given him a perseverance and a fortitude he'd thought lost; now he realized that his energy was running out and that, unless another miracle occurred or someone helped him, his adventure would very soon be at an end. After a while, when he felt a little restored and the sun shining through the foliage had instilled in him a scrap of optimism, he gathered all his strength, stood up and started walking towards the farm.

Maria Ferré would never forget the radiant February dawn she first set eyes on Rafael Sánchez Mazas. Her parents were out in the field and she was getting ready to feed the cows when a man appeared in the yard – tall, famished and spectral, with his twisted spectacles and many days' growth of beard, in his sheepskin jacket and trousers full of holes, and covered in mud and weeds – and asked her for a piece of bread. Maria wasn't scared. She'd just turned twenty-six and she was a dark blonde, illiterate, hard-working girl for whom the war was nothing more than a confusing background noise to the letters her brother sent home from the front, and a meaningless whirlwind that two years earlier had taken the life of a boy from Palol de Revardit she'd once dreamed of marrying.

During this time her family hadn't been hungry or frightened, because the farm lands they cultivated and the cows, pigs and hens sheltering in the stables were enough, more than enough, to feed them, and because, although Mas Borrell, their house, was located halfway between Palol de Revardit and Cornellà de Terri, the abuses of the days of revolution didn't reach them and the disorder of the retreat brought them only the odd lost, disarmed soldier who, more frightened than threatening, asked for something to eat or stole a hen. It's possible that at first Sánchez Mazas was to Maria Ferré just another of the many deserters who roamed the area during those days, and that's why she wasn't scared, but she always maintained that as soon as she saw his pitiful figure outlined against the ground of the path that ran past the yard, she recognized beneath the ravages of three days' exposure to the elements the unmistakable bearing of a gentleman. Whether that's true or not, Maria gave the man the same kind treatment she'd given countless other fugitives.

'I don't have any bread,' she told him. 'But I could heat something up for you.'

Undone by gratitude, Sánchez Mazas followed her into the kitchen and, while Maria heated up the previous night's saucepan – where, in a rich, brown broth, floated lentils and big chunks of bacon, sausage and chorizo along with potatoes and vegetables – he sat down on a bench, enjoying the nearness of the fire and the joyful promise of hot food, took off his soaking shoes and socks, and suddenly noticed a terrible ache in his feet and an infinite tiredness in his bony shoulders. Maria handed him a clean rag and some clogs, and out of the corner of her eye watched him dry his neck, his face, his hair, as well as his feet and ankles, while watching the flames dance amid the logs with staring, slightly glazed eyes, and when she handed him the food she saw him devour it with a hunger of many days, in silence and scarcely forgoing the manners of a man raised among linen tablecloths and silver cutlery, which, more out of his courteous instincts than his recently acquired habit of fear, made him set the spoon and pewter plate down by the fire and stand up when Maria's parents burst into the half-light of the kitchen and stood, looking at him, with a bovine mixture of passivity and suspicion. Perhaps mistakenly thinking their guest didn't understand Catalan, Maria told her father in Catalan what had happened; he asked Sánchez Mazas to finish his meal and, without taking his eyes off him, put his farming tools down beside a stone bench, washed his hands in a basin and came over to the fire. As he sensed the father approach, Sánchez Mazas scraped the plate clean. His hunger calmed, he'd reached a decision: he realized that, if he didn't reveal his true identity, he wouldn't have the slightest chance of being offered shelter there either, and he also realized that the hypothetical risk of denunciation was preferable to the real risk of starving or freezing to death.

'My name is Rafael Sánchez Mazas and I am the most senior living leader of the Falange in Spain,' he finally said to the man who listened without looking at him.

Sixty years later, when neither her parents nor Sánchez Mazas were alive to do so, Maria still recalled those words exactly, perhaps because that was the first time she'd heard of the Falange, just as she recalled that Sánchez Mazas went on to relate his implausible adventure at Collell, told them about his wanderings of the last few days and, addressing the man, added:

'You know as well as I do that the Nationalists will be here any time now. It's a question of days, if not hours. But if the reds catch me I'm a dead man. Believe me, I'm very grateful for your hospitality, and I wouldn't want to take advantage of your good faith, but if you could give me what your daughter just gave me to eat once a day and a sheltered spot to spend the night, I shall be eternally grateful. Think it over. If you do me this favour you'll be well rewarded.'

Maria Ferré's father didn't need to think it over. He assured him that he could not have him in the house because it would be too risky, but he proposed a better alternative: Sánchez Mazas would spend the day in the woods, in a safe field nearby beside the Mas de la Casa Nova – a farm abandoned by its owners since the beginning of the war – and at night he would sleep warmly in a hayloft, a couple of hundred metres from the house, where they would make sure he didn't lack food. Sánchez Mazas was delighted with the plan, he took the blanket and package of food Maria prepared for him, took his leave of her and her mother, and followed her father along the dirt track that passed in front of the door to the house and then went along through sown fields the top of which – through the clear air of the sunny morning – overlooked the road to Banyoles and the valley full of farms and further off the jagged, distant profile of the Pyrenees. After a while, once Maria's father had pointed out in the distance the hayloft where he should spend the night, they crossed an open, uncultivated field and stopped at the edge of the woods, just where the track thinned out into a narrow path; the man then told him that at the end of the path was the Mas de la Casa Nova and insisted he not return until night had fallen. Sánchez Mazas didn't have time even to reiterate his gratitude, because the man turned and started walking back towards Mas Borrell. Following his instructions, Sánchez Mazas entered a forest of ash trees, holly and enormously tall oaks which barely let the sun through and got thicker and more impenetrable as the path went down the slope of a hillside, and he'd been walking for long enough for a little voice to start injecting him with the venom of mistrust when he came out into a clearing in the middle of which stood the Mas de la Casa Nova. It was a two-storey stone farmhouse, with an artesian well and a big wooden door; once he was sure it had been uninhabited for a long time Sánchez Mazas considered forcing one of the entrances and holing up inside, but after a moment of reflection he decided to follow Maria Ferré's father's instructions and look for the field he'd recommended. He found it quite nearby, as soon as he crossed a steep, rocky, dry streambed lined with elms, and he lay down there, in the tall grass, under the clear, perfectly blue sky and the dazzling sun that warmed the cold, still morning air, and although every bone in his body ached with exhaustion and an endless fatigue weighed down his eyelids, for the first time in a long time he felt safe and almost happy, reconciled with reality, and as he noticed the pleasant weight of sunlight on his eyes and skin and the irrevocable slipping of his consciousness towards the waters of sleep, like an anomalous offshoot of that unforeseen plenitude, some lines appeared on his lips that he didn't even remember having read:

Do not move
Let the wind speak
That is paradise

Hours later, anxiety awakened him. The sun shone in the middle of the sky and although he still had a twinge of pain in his muscles, sleep had restored part of his energy and strength that he'd burnt-up over the last few days in the desperation to cling to life; but as soon as he got free of Maria Ferré's blanket and heard in the silence of the field a distant noise of many running motors he realized the cause of his uneasiness. He went to the far edge of the field and from there, needlessly hidden, he watched from afar the procession of a large column of trucks and Republican soldiers swarming along the Banyoles road. Although in the immediate future he'd experience the threatening proximity of enemy troops many more times, only that morning did he consider it a danger, and feel he must return to his improvised bed, collect the blanket and package of food, and duck into the edge of the forest to hide. There, in a shelter made of stone and branches, which he planned that very afternoon but didn't start building until the following dawn, he spent most of the next three days. At first the construction of the shelter kept him busy, but then time went by as he lay on the ground sometimes sleeping, recouping the energy that he could see he might need at any moment, searching through his memory for every forgotten instant of his wartime adventure and especially imagining how he would tell it once he was liberated by his own people – a liberation that the logic of events brought ever nearer, yet his impatience made him feel was ever further away. He didn't talk to anyone except Maria Ferré or her father, with whom he'd chat for a while in the hayloft when they came in the dark to bring him food, and on the only night when her father allowed him to come inside and have dinner with them he also talked to two Republican deserters the family knew, and who, as they ate a little and warmed up by the fire before continuing their journey to Banyoles, told him the Nationalist troops had entered Gerona that morning.

The following day passed as usual; on the next everything changed. As he had every morning, Sánchez Mazas got up with the sun, picked up the package of food they'd brought him from Mas Borrell and started walking towards Mas de la Casa Nova; as he was crossing the streambed, he tripped and fell. He didn't hurt himself, but he broke his glasses. The event, which under normal circumstances would have inconvenienced him, now drove him to despair: he was extremely short-sighted and, without the help of corrective lenses, reality was nothing but an unintelligible handful of smudges. Sitting on the ground, with his broken spectacles in his hands, he cursed his clumsiness; he was on the point of weeping with rage. Pulling himself together, he crawled up the bank of the stream on all fours, and feeling his way, guided by the routine of the last few days, searched out the shelter by the field.

That was when he heard the order to halt. Stopping dead and instinctively putting his hands up, he made out at a distance of fifteen metres, barely distinguishable against the confusing green of the woods, three cloudy figures starting to advance towards him with an expectant, watchful attitude. When they were closer Sánchez Mazas realized they were Republican soldiers, they were very young, and they were pointing two long-barrelled nine-millimetre pistols at him; they were as nervous and startled as he was, and their shabby fugitive air and the undisciplined disparity of their uniforms made him assume they were deserters, but he didn't have time to figure out a way of confirming his suspicion because the one who spoke for them submitted him to an interrogation which lasted for almost half an hour of tension, guesswork and insinuations, until Sánchez Mazas resolved that this fortuitous encounter, just after breaking his glasses, could only be a favourable play of fate and decided to put all his money on it and admit that he'd spent six days wandering in the woods waiting for the arrival of the Nationalists.

This confession resolved the misunderstanding. Because although the three soldiers' adventure had only just begun, their motives were identical to those of Sánchez Mazas. Two of them were the Figueras brothers, Pere and Joachim; the other was called Daniel Angelats. Pere was the oldest of the three, and the most capable and most intelligent. Although in adolescence he'd been unable to convince his father – a devious but very respected businessman in Cornellà de Terri – to pay for him to study law in Barcelona and he'd had to stay in the village helping the family in their small garlic business, since he was a child his indiscriminately eager reading (first in the school library and later in the *Ateneo Popular*) had refined his understanding and given him an uncommon range of knowledge. The collective enthusiasm awakened by the proclamation of the Republic attracted his attention towards politics, but it wasn't until after the events of October 1934 that he became a member of the Catalan Republican Left, and the uprising of the summer of 1936 caught him finishing his military service in an infantry barracks in Pedralbes, where on 19 July, earlier than usual, they were woken up with an untimely ration of cognac at breakfast and the announcement that they were going to march through Barcelona that morning in honour of the Popular Olympiad; nevertheless, before noon he'd already gone over, with weapons and equipment, along with other soldiers of his detachment, to a column of anarchist workers who urged them to join their ranks on an avenue in the city centre. During the entire afternoon and night of that dreadful Monday he fought in the streets to put down the rebellion, and in the revolutionary delirium of the days that followed, exasperated by the timidity of the government of the Generalitat, he joined the libertarian onrush of the Durruti column and went off to recapture Zaragoza. But, since neither the intoxication of victory over the rebels nor the idealistic vehemence of much of his reading had completely overridden his Catalan peasant's common sense, he soon sensed his error; once convinced by events that it was impossible to win a war with an army of enthusiastic amateurs, at the first opportunity he joined the regular army of the Republic. Under its discipline he fought at Madrid's University City and in the Maestrazgo, but at the beginning of May 1938 a stray bullet cleanly pierced his thigh and afforded him some months of convalescence, first in improvised field hospitals and finally in the military hospital in Gerona. There, amid the end of the world disorder reigning in the city during the days of retreat, his mother came for him. Although he'd just turned twenty-five, Pere Figueras was by then an old man, tired and disillusioned, in a bit of a daze, but he didn't even have a limp any more, so he was able to follow his mother back home. To his surprise, waiting for him in Can Pigem, together with his sisters, were his brother Joaquim and Daniel Angelats, who that very morning had taken advantage of the terror and confusion spread by a bomb that landed on the Grober factory in Gerona, near where they'd stopped to refuel, in order to evade the vigilance of the political commissar of their company and escape through the old part of the city towards Cornellà de Terri. Joaquim and Angelats had met two years earlier when, barely nineteen years old, they were recruited and, after three months' military instruction in the Sanctuary of Collell, sent as members of the Garibaldi Brigade to the Aragón front. Their inexperience saved them from much unpleasantness: that and the impression they gave of being adolescents too young for combat got them sent immediately back to the rearguard – first to Binéfar and later to Barcelona and finally to Vilanova i la Geltrú, where they joined a coastal artillery battalion made up mostly of wounded and disabled soldiers, where for months they played at war; but when the Republic felt its fate was at stake on the beaches of the Ebro, even they were sent as a last hope to contain, with their old, inefficient cannon, the Nationalist onslaught. The front collapsed and the rout began; all along the Mediterranean coast the shredded remains of the Republican army were retreating in disarray towards the border, unceasingly harassed by gunfire from the German planes and by the constant encircling manoeuvres of Yagüe, Solchaga and Gambara, who hemmed into inescapable pockets (or with no escape but the sea) hundreds of prisoners terrified by the shrieks of the Moroccan regulars. Bereft of political convictions, starving, defeated and sick of war, unwilling to face the agony of exile, persuaded by Francoist propaganda that, unless their hands were stained with blood, they had nothing to fear from the victors except the restoration of the order the Republic had shattered, Figueras and Angelats had no other ambition by this point than to save their skins, evade the limitless fury of the Moors and take advantage of their commanders' slightest distraction to take the road home and wait there for the arrival of the Nationalists.

So they did. But the very afternoon they arrived at the Figueras home, something happened to convince them that the big house on the edge of the Banyoles highway and right across from the train station was not a safe haven for deserters. While they were badgered with questions by the family as they sated their ravenous hunger along with Pere Figueras, before they had taken off their soldiers' uniforms, they heard the sound of motors stopping in front of Can Pigem. According to Joaquim Figueras, it was his mother who, guessing the danger they were in, urged them to go upstairs and hide under the enormous bed in the master bedroom. From there they heard a knock on the door, then unfamiliar voices conversing in the dining room that had been swiftly cleared, and then the noise of military boots climbing the stairs and walking around the second floor until they saw them come into the room; there were two pairs: one, which stayed in the doorway, was cracked and dusty; the other, old but recently shined, still martial, clicked a bit over the floor tiles until the Figueras brothers and Angelats, holding their breath under the bed, heard a soft, commanding voice ask that the room be prepared for him to spend the night. As soon as they were alone again, the three deserters almost wordlessly took the only decision possible and, instinctively persuaded that only speed could make up for the obligatory recklessness of the manoeuvre, they crawled out of their hiding place and, without looking up and trying to prevent the rigidity of their movements from betraying their hurry, went down the stairs, crossed the kitchen and yard and highway protected by the anonymity of their uniforms, which camouflaged them among all the other soldiers in the house or around the house waiting their turn to eat, or resting or arranging their things, calmly resigned to their stateless futures.

From that afternoon on the Figueras brothers and Angelats went into hiding. Undoubtedly it wasn't as hard for them as for Sánchez Mazas: they were young, they were armed, they knew the area and many people in the area; not only that but as soon as the Republican detachment left Cam Pigem the next morning, the Figueras' mother began to provide them with food in abundance and lots of warm clothing and blankets. They spent the daylight hours in the woods, not far from Cornellà de Terri or from the Banyoles highway, always alert to the troop movements along it, and at night they slept in an abandoned barn near the Mas de la Casa Nova. It seems incredible they didn't bump into Sánchez Mazas until they'd been installed (the word is of course excessive) for three days in the vicinity of the Mas de la Casa Nova, since they'd arrived the same day as he had, but that's how it was. Sixty years later, Joaquim Figueras and Daniel Angelats both still remembered with absolute clarity the morning they saw him for the first time: the sound of breaking branches that alarmed them in the silence of the forest, and then the willowy, blind figure in the sheepskin jacket with the shattered spectacles in his hand, feeling his way up the rocky, tangled bank of the stream. They also remembered the moment they stopped him at gunpoint and the minutes of interminable reckoning and suspicion during which they, as much as Sánchez Mazas – whose attitude during this first conversation or interrogation drifted imperceptibly from frightened and dishonourable pleading to the almost paternalistic aplomb of one who knows himself to be beyond his interlocutor not only in years but especially in intellect and guile – tried to find out the intentions of the other; and that, as soon as they did, Sánchez Mazas identified himself, offering them exorbitant rewards if they helped him cross the lines. Joaquim Figueras and Daniel Angelats also agree on another point: as soon as Sánchez Mazas said his name, Pere Figueras knew who he was. Although this might seem strange, it is not absolutely implausible: for quite a few years by then, Sánchez Mazas had been known all over Spain as a writer and politician and, although Pere Figueras had barely left his village except to defend the Republic with bullets, he could easily have seen his name and photograph in the newspapers and could have read articles he'd written. In any case, Pere, who had taken charge of the trio of soldiers without anyone telling him to, told him they couldn't take him to the other side, but said he could stay with them until the Nationalists arrived. Implicitly or explicitly, the pact was this: now they would protect him, with their weapons and their youth and their knowledge of the area and the people of the area, and later he would protect them with his indisputable authority as a hierarch. The offer was not up for discussion, and although Joaquim at first put up a bit of resistance to the idea of taking on, in those uncertain days, the responsibility of a half-blind man who, if they were captured by the Republicans, would earn them immediate execution, in the end he had no choice but to submit to his brother's will.

The life of the three deserters didn't change in any noticeable way after that moment, except for the fact that now there were four to feed from what the Figueras' mother sent, and four to sleep in the abandoned barn by Mas de la Casa Nova, for they decided that it was safer for Sánchez Mazas not to return to the hayloft by Mas Borrell. Curiously (or maybe not: maybe it's life's decisive moments that are most voraciously devoured by oblivion), neither Joaquim Figueras nor Daniel Angelats have a very clear memory of those days. Figueras, whose memory is sharp but expeditious and often gets lost in aimless meandering, remembers that meeting Sánchez Mazas relieved the boredom for a while, because he told them his wartime adventures, with a wealth of detail and in a tone that had at first impressed him with its solemnity but with time he'd come to consider a little pompous; he also remembered that, once they'd told their war stories – undoubtedly in a much more succinct, disorderly and direct manner – they were again overtaken by the tense, impatient boredom they'd suffered for the last few days. Or he and Daniel Angelats were at least. Because what Joaquim Figueras does remember very well is that, while he and Angelats went back to practising the most varied ways of killing time much as before, his brother Pere and Sánchez Mazas leaned up against the trunk of an oak tree at the edge of the woods conversing tirelessly. He could see them there still: listless and unshaven and well bundled up, with their knees higher and higher and their heads lower and lower as the day wore on, almost with their backs to each other, smoking cut tobacco or whittling away at something, turning to look at each other every now and then and, of course, not smiling at all, as if neither of the two were looking to the other for agreement or persuasion, but only the certainty that none of his words would be lost in the air. He never knew what they were talking about, or maybe he didn't want to know; he knew the subject was not politics or the war; once he suspected (without much basis) that it was literature. The truth is Joaquim Figueras, who'd never got along very well with Pere (whom he'd made fun of publicly more than once and whom he'd always secretly admired), realized with a secret pang of jealousy that Sánchez Mazas won, in a few hours, a friendship with his brother that he'd never had access to in his whole life. As for Angelats, whose memory is shakier than Figueras', his testimony does not contradict that of his old friend; at best, it complements it with various anecdotal details (Angelats, for example, remembers Sánchez Mazas writing with a minuscule pencil in his notebook with dark green covers, which perhaps proves that the diary was written during the events it relates) and one detail perhaps less so. As often happens with the memories of some old people which, because they are about to be left without them, remember much more clearly a childhood afternoon than what happened a few hours ago, in this concrete point Angelats' abounds in particulars. I don't know if time has given the scene a novelistic varnish; although I can't be sure, I tend to think not, because I know Angelats is a man without imagination; nor does any benefit occur to me that he might derive – a tired and ill man, with few years left to live – from inventing such a scene.

This is the scene:

At some point during the second night the four of them spent together in the barn, Angelats was awakened by a noise. Startled, he sat up and saw Joaquim Figueras sleeping placidly beside him among the straw and blankets; Pere and Sánchez Mazas weren't there. He was about to get up (or wake Joaquim, who was less of a coward or at least more decisive than he was) when he heard voices and realised that was what had woken him; they were barely whispering but their words carried to him clearly in the perfect silence of the barn, on the other side of which, almost level with the floor and beside the half-closed door, Angelats saw the glow of two cigarettes burning in the darkness. He told himself that Pere and Sánchez Mazas had left the straw bed where the four of them slept to smoke safely; he then wondered what time it was and, imagining Pere and Sánchez Mazas had been awake and talking for a long while, lay back down and tried to fall asleep again. He couldn't. Sleepless, he clung on to the thread of conversation between the two insomniacs: at first uninterestedly, just to while away the time, for he understood the words he was hearing but not their meaning nor their intention; then things changed. Angelats heard the voice of Sánchez Mazas, deep and deliberate, slightly hoarse, telling of the days in Collell, the hours, the minutes, the frightful seconds that preceded and followed the shooting; Angelats knew of the episode because Sánchez Mazas had told them of it the first morning they were together, but now, perhaps because the impenetrable darkness of the barn and the careful choice of words conferred on the events an additional reality, he heard as if for the first time or as if, more than hearing it, he

112

was reliving it, expectant and with his heart contracted, perhaps a little incredulous, because also for the first time – Sánchez Mazas had avoided mentioning him in the first telling – he saw the militiaman standing beside the ditch, in the rain, tall and burly and soaked through, looking at Sánchez Mazas with his grey, perhaps greenish, eyes under the double arch of his brows, his gaunt cheeks and prominent cheekbones, silhouetted against the dark green of the pines and the dark blue of the clouds, panting a little, his large hands grasping the slanted rifle and the field uniform with all its buckles, threadbare from exposure. He was very young, Angelats heard Sánchez Mazas say. Your age or perhaps younger, although he had an adult expression and features. For a moment, while he looked at me, I thought I knew who he was; now I'm sure. There was a silence, as if Sánchez Mazas was waiting for Pere's question, which didn't come; Angelats made out at the end of the barn the glow of two cigarettes, one grew momentarily more intense and lit up Pere's face with a weak reddish radiance. He wasn't a Carabinero or a SIM agent, obviously, Sánchez Mazas went on. Had he been, I'd not be here now. No: he was a simple soldier. Like you. Or like your brother. One of the ones who guarded us when we went out walking in the garden. I noticed him straightaway and I think he noticed me too, or at least that's what I think now, because in reality we never exchanged a single word. But I noticed him, as did all my companions, he was always sitting on a bench humming something, popular songs and things like that, and one afternoon he stood up from the bench and began to sing 'Sighing for Spain'. Have you ever heard it? Of course, said Pere. It's Liliana's favourite paso doble, said Sánchez

Mazas. I always think it's so sad, but her feet start up if she hears four notes of it. We've danced to it so many times . . . Angelats saw the ash of Sánchez Mazas' cigarette redden and then go out abruptly, and then he heard him raise his hoarse and almost ironic voice in a whisper and recognized in the silence of the night the melody and lyrics of the paso doble, which made him feel so much like weeping because they suddenly struck him as the saddest lyrics and music in the world, as well as a desolate mirror of his wasted youth and the pitiful future awaiting him: 'God desired, in his power, / to blend four little sunbeams / and make of them a woman, / and when His will was done / in a Spanish garden I was born / like a flower on her rose-bush. / Glorious land of my love, / blessed land of perfume and passion, / Spain, in each flower at your feet / a heart is sighing. / Oh, I'm dying of sorrow, / for I'm going away, Spain, from you, / for away from my rose-bush I'm torn.' Sánchez Mazas stopped his soft singing. Do you know all of it? asked Pere. All of what? asked Sánchez Mazas. The song, answered Pere. More or less, answered Sánchez Mazas. There was another silence. So, said Pere. And what happened with the soldier? Nothing, said Sánchez Mazas. Instead of sitting on the bench, humming quietly like usual, that afternoon he started singing 'Sighing for Spain' out loud, smiling and, as if he were letting himself be swept away by an invisible force, he stood up and started to dance through the garden with his eyes closed, embracing his rifle as if it were a woman, in the same way, just as gently, and I and my companions and the rest of the soldiers who were guarding us and even the Carabineros stopped and stared, sadly or dumbfounded or mocking, but all in silence while he dragged his big military boots over the gravel riddled with cigarette butts and bits of food, just as if they were leather shoes on a pristine dance floor – and then, before he'd finished dancing to the song, someone said his name and cursed him affectionately and the spell was broken, a lot of men started laughing or smiling; we laughed, prisoners and guards, everyone . . . I think it was the first time I had laughed in a long, long time. Sánchez Mazas fell quiet. Angelats heard Joaquim roll over beside him, and wondered if he might be listening too, but the rough, regular breathing soon made him discard the notion. That was it? asked Pere. That was it, answered Sánchez Mazas. Are you sure it was him? asked Pere. Yes, answered Sánchez Mazas. I think so. What was his name? asked Pere. You said someone said his name. I don't know, answered Sánchez Mazas. Perhaps I didn't hear. Or I heard it and I forgot it straightaway. But it was him. I wonder why he didn't give me away, why he let me escape. I've asked myself over and over again. They grew quiet again, and Angelats felt that this time the silence was denser and longer, and thought the conversation had finished. He was looking at me for a moment from the edge of the ditch, Sánchez Mazas continued. He looked at me strangely, no one has ever looked at me like that, as if he'd known me for a long time but at that moment was unable to recognize me and was making an effort to do so, or like an entomologist who doesn't know whether he has a unique and unknown specimen before him, or like someone trying in vain to decipher an elusive secret from the shape of a cloud. But no: in reality the way he looked at me was . . . joyful. Joyful? asked Pere. Yes, said Sánchez Mazas. Joyful. I don't understand, said Pere. Me neither, said Sánchez Mazas.

Well, he added after another pause, I don't know. I think I'm talking nonsense. It must be very late, said Pere. We'd better try to get some sleep. Yes, said Sánchez Mazas. Angelats heard them get up, lie down in the straw side by side, next to Joaquim, and also heard them (or maybe just imagined them) trying in vain to get to sleep, tossing and turning in the blankets, unable to get free of the song that had become tangled up in their memories, and the image of that soldier dancing with his rifle in his arms among the cypress trees and prisoners, in the garden at Collell.

That happened on the Thursday night; the next day the Nationalists arrived. Since Tuesday the last military convoys had been passing continually and they had heard explosion after explosion as the Republicans – blowing up bridges, cutting communications – tried to protect their retreat; and so Sánchez Mazas and his three companions spent the whole of Friday morning impatiently keeping watch over the highway from their observatory in the field, until just after noon they spotted the first Nationalist scouts. The group erupted with joy. However, before going to meet their liberators, Sánchez Mazas convinced them to accompany him to Mas Borrell to thank Maria Ferré and her family, and when they arrived at Mas Borrell they found Maria Ferré's father and her mother, but not Maria Ferré. She clearly remembers at noon on that day, from a spot not far from where Sánchez Mazas and his companions were, she had also seen the first Nationalist troops go by and after a while a neighbour had come to tell her on behalf of her parents that she should go back home, because there were soldiers in her house. Slightly worried, Maria started walking alongside her neighbour, but she calmed down when her neighbour told her that the lads from Can Pigem were amongst the soldiers. Although she'd not exchanged more than four words with Pere or Joaquim, she'd known them all her life, and as soon as she saw the younger Figueras in the farmyard, chatting with Angelats, she recognized him immediately. In the kitchen were Pere and Sánchez Mazas with her parents; euphoric, Sánchez Mazas embraced her, lifted her up in the air, kissed her. Then he told the Ferrés what had happened during the days they'd had no news of him, and showering Angelats and the Figueras brothers with words of praise and gratitude, he said:

'Now we're friends.' Neither Maria nor Joaquim Figueras remember, but Angelats does: it was at this moment when, according to him, Sánchez Mazas pronounced, for the first time, the words he would repeat many times in the years to come and that until the ends of their lives would resonate in the memories of the lads who helped him survive, the words that had the adventurous ring of a secret password: 'The forest friends'. And, again according to Angelats, he added with a touch of solemnity: 'One day I'll tell the whole story in a book; it'll be called *Soldiers of Salamis*.'

Before leaving, he reiterated his eternal gratitude to the Ferrés for having harboured him, and begged them not to hesitate to get in touch with him if there was ever anything they thought he might be able to help them with, and by way of a safe-conduct, in case they had any problems with the new authorities, he wrote down plainly on a piece of paper what they'd done for him. Then they left, and from the back door Maria and her parents watched them go off down the dirt track in the direction of Cornellà, Sánchez Mazas in the lead – tall and proud like a captain in charge of the negligible, elated, shabby remains of his victorious troops – Joaquim and Angelats escorting him, and Pere a little further back and almost downcast, as if he wasn't entirely sharing the joy of the others but would battle with all his strength so as not to be excluded from it. Over the following years, Maria would write to Sánchez Mazas many times and he would always answer in his own handwriting. Sánchez Mazas' letters no longer exist, because Maria, on the advice of her mother, who for some reason feared they might compromise her, eventually destroyed them. As for her own letters, the secretary of the Banyoles Town Hall wrote them for her, and in them she asked for relatives, friends or acquaintances to be released from prison, which they almost invariably were; so over the years she was endowed with a saint's halo, or made into a fairy godmother to the desperate people of the region, whose families came in search of protection for the indiscriminate victims of a post-war period that in those days no one could have imagined would last so long. Other than her family, no one else knew that the source of those favours wasn't a secret lover of Maria's, or a supernatural power she'd always had but hadn't thought appropriate to use until now, but rather a fugitive beggar she'd offered a little hot food one day at dawn and whom, after that mid-morning in February when he disappeared down the dirt track in the company of the Figueras brothers and Angelats, she never saw again in her entire life.

Sánchez Mazas spent some time at Can Pigem waiting for transportation to take him back to Barcelona. They were very happy days. Although in some parts of Spain the war continued its course, for him and for his companions it was over, and the terrible memory of those months of uncertainty, captivity and the proximity of death reinforced his euphoria, as did the anticipation of his imminent reunion with his family and friends and with the new country he'd decisively contributed to forging. Eager to ingratiate itself with the new authorities – and the new authorities being eager to ingratiate themselves with the people – that militantly Republican region celebrated the entrance of the Nationalists in style, with feasts and fairs never lacking the presence of Sánchez Mazas and his three companions, still dressed in their Popular Army uniforms and carrying their long-barrelled nine-millimetre pistols, but especially protected by the intimidating presence of the hierarch, who a little ironically but unfailingly introduced them as his personal guard. This period of cheerful impunity ended for them the morning that a lieutenant of a column of regulars burst into Can Pigem, announcing that a car leaving immediately for Barcelona had a free seat for Sánchez Mazas. Without even time to take his leave of the Figueras or Angelats families, Sánchez Mazas managed to hand Pere the notebook with the green covers where, as well as the diary of his days in the forest, he'd put down in writing the bond of gratitude that would always unite them, and Joaquim Figueras and Daniel Angelats remember very well that the last words they heard him say, reaching out a hand to wave goodbye from the window of the car that was already on its way down the Gerona highway, were:

'We'll meet again!'

But Sánchez Mazas was mistaken: he never saw Pere or Joaquim Figueras again, nor Daniel Angelats. However, and although Sánchez Mazas never came to find out, Daniel Angelats and Joaquim Figueras did see him again.

It happened several months later, in Zaragoza. Sánchez Mazas was then a completely different man from the one they'd known. Driven by the momentum of the liberation, in those days he was tirelessly active: he'd visited Barcelona, Burgos, Salamanca, Bilbao, Rome, San Sebastián; everywhere he was the object of lavish hospitality, celebrating his liberty and incorporation into Nationalist Spain as if it were a triumph of incalculable value to its future; everywhere he wrote articles, gave interviews, lectures, speeches and radio broadcasts where he'd make veiled allusions to episodes during his long period in custody and where, with a cohesive faith, he placed himself at the service of the new regime. Nevertheless, from the day after he left Can Pigem and began visiting the office of Dionisio Ridruejo (Chief of Press and Propaganda for the rebels) where he regularly met with his intellectual Falangist comrades, both new and old, Sánchez Mazas could have sensed, in and among the triumphalist atmosphere of superficial fraternity, the suspicions and mistrust among the victors that Franco's guile and three years of conspiratorial secret meetings in the rearguard had caused. He could have sensed it, but he didn't – or didn't want to. This is easily explained: having recently recovered his liberty, Sánchez Mazas thought everything had turned out perfectly, because he couldn't imagine that the reality of Franco's Spain differed one iota from his desires; that was not the case for some of his old Falangist comrades. Ever since the proclamation on 19 April 1937 of the Decree of Unification, a veritable *coup d'état* in reverse (as Ridruejo would call it years later), by which all political forces that had joined the Uprising came to be integrated in one single party under the command of the

Generalísimo, the old guard of the Falange began to suspect the fascist revolution they'd dreamt of was never going to happen. In fact the expeditious cocktail of its doctrine – which blended, in a brilliant, demagogic and impossible amalgam, both the preservation of certain traditional values with the urgency for profound change in the social and economic structures of the country, and the terror the middle classes felt of the proletarian revolution with a vitalist Nietzschean irrationalism, which, faced with inherent bourgeois prudence, advocated the romance of living dangerously – would eventually be diluted into sanctimonious, predictable, conservative slop. By 1937, beheaded by José Antonio's death, domesticated as an ideology and annulled as an apparatus of power, the Falange, with its rhetoric and its rites and the rest of its external fascist manifestations, was already available to Franco to use as an instrument to bring his regime into line with Hitler's Germany and Mussolini's Italy (from which he'd received and was receiving and still hoped to receive so much aid), but Franco could also use it, as José Antonio had foreseen and feared years before, 'as a mere auxiliary shock element, like an assault guard of reaction, like a youthful militia destined to parade before the upraised bigheads in power'. Everything conspired in those years to dilute the original Falange, from the orthopaedic use Franco made of it, to the crucial fact that over the course of the war not only did those who shared its ideology to a fair degree join on a massive scale but also those who sought, within its ranks, to hide their Republican pasts. Things being as they were, the choice that sooner or later many 'old shirts' had to face was clear: denounce the flagrant discrepancy between their political project and that governing the new state, or coexist as comfortably as they could with this contradiction and apply themselves to scraping up even the tiniest crumbs from the banquet of power. Of course, between these two extremes the intermediate positions were almost infinite; but the truth of the matter is that, in spite of so much invented honesty professed after the fact, except for Ridruejo – a man who erred many times, but who was almost always unsullied and brave and pure as pure – almost no one opted openly for the first.

Naturally, Sánchez Mazas did not. Not right after the war finished, or ever. But on 9 April 1939, eighteen days before Pere Figueras and his eight comrades from Cornellà de Terri were imprisoned in Gerona and the same day that Ramón Serrano Súñer – at the time Minister of the Interior, Franco's brother-in-law and the Falangists' principal sentinel in government – organized and presided over an act of homage to Sánchez Mazas in Zaragoza, he still had no serious reason to imagine that the country he had aspired to create was not the same as the one the new regime aspired to create; much less did he suspect that Joaquim Figueras and Daniel Angelats were also in Zaragoza. As a matter of fact, they had spent barely a month in the city, where they'd been sent to fulfil their military service, when they heard on the radio that Sánchez Mazas had been staying in the Grand Hotel since the previous day and that night he was going to give a speech to the top brass of the Aragonese Falange. In part out of curiosity, but mostly driven by hope that Sánchez Mazas' influence could do something to relieve the rigours of their privates' barracks regime, Figueras and Angelats showed up at the Grand Hotel and told a porter they were friends of Sánchez Mazas and would like to see him. Figueras still remembers that placid, corpulent porter very well, with his blue frock coat with tassels and fancy gold fastenings gleaming under the foyer's crystal chandeliers, amid the constant coming and going of uniformed hierarchs, and especially his expression halfway between sarcasm and disbelief as he looked over their miserable uniforms and irredeemably rustic appearance. Finally, the porter told them that Sánchez Mazas was in his room, resting, and that he wasn't authorized to disturb him or to let them through.

'But you lads can wait for him here,' he spoke down to them with a twinge of cruelty, pointing at some chairs. 'When he comes down, break through the cordon the Falangists will form and greet him: if he recognizes you, great, but if he doesn't recognize you . . .' smiling grimly, he ran his index finger across his throat.

'We'll wait,' Figueras proudly parried, dragging Angelats over to a chair.

They waited for almost two hours, but as the time passed they felt more and more intimidated by the porter's warning, the unheard-of sumptuousness of the hotel, the asphyxiating fascist paraphernalia with which it was decorated, and by the time the foyer finally filled up with military greetings and blue shirts and red berets, Figueras and Angelats had given up on their original intention and decided to go straight back to the barracks without approaching Sánchez Mazas. They hadn't yet left the foyer when a Falangist guard of honour formed between the stairway and the revolving door and blocked their way and, a little later, allowed them a brief glimpse for the last time in their lives, gliding along with the projected martial manner of a *condottiere* among a sea of red berets and a forest of raised arms, of the unmistakable Jewish profile of that man, his prestige now enhanced by the prosopopeia of power – who three months before, diminished by rags and unseeing eyes, by exhaustion, privations and fear, had implored their help in a remote and empty field – and who could now never repay that wartime favour to two of his forest friends.

The Zaragoza function, during which he delivered his 'Saturday of Glory' speech – in which, undoubtedly because he already sensed the danger of defections, he exasperatedly called his Falangist comrades to discipline and blind obedience to the Caudillo – was just one more of Sánchez Mazas' numerous public contributions during those months. Since Ledesma Ramos, José Antonio and Ruiz de Alda had been shot at the beginning of the war, Sánchez Mazas was the most senior living member of the Falange; this, added to his brotherly friendship with José Antonio and the crucial role he'd had in the early Falange, gave him an enormous influence over his colleagues in the party, and persuaded Franco to treat him with the greatest consideration, to win his loyalty and to smooth over the bitterness that had arisen in his relationship with some of the less accommodating Falangists. The culmination of this simple yet extremely effective strategy of recruitment, similar in every respect to a bribe of perks and praises – a method, it's worth noting, the Caudillo wielded like a virtuoso and to which a good part of his interminable monopoly of power can be attributed – took place in August 1939, when, in putting together the first post-war government, Sánchez Mazas, who since May had occupied the position of

124

National Delegate of the *Falange Exterior*, was named Minister Without Portfolio. This was not, of course, an exclusive occupation, or he didn't take it very seriously; in any case, he knew how to fulfil it without any prejudice to his recaptured vocation as a writer: during that time he published frequently in newspapers and journals, attended literary gatherings and gave public readings, and in February 1940 he was elected a member of the Royal Academy of the Spanish Language, along with his friend Eugenio Montes, as 'spokesman for the poetry and revolutionary language of the Falange', according to the daily newspaper *ABC*. Sánchez Mazas was a vain man, but not stupid, so his vanity did not overrule his pride: aware that his election to the Academy obeyed political rather than literary motives, he never actually delivered his acceptance speech for admission into the institution. Other factors must have had a hand in this gesture that everyone has chosen to interpret, not without reason, as an elegant sign of the writer's disdain for mundane glories. Although it too has always been seen as such, it is a riskier proposition attributing the same significance to one of the episodes that contributed most to endowing Sánchez Mazas' figure with the aristocratic aureole of unconcern and indolence that surrounded him till his death.

The legend, proclaimed to the four winds by the most diverse sources, has it that one day in July 1940, during a full Council of Ministers, Franco, fed up with Sánchez Mazas not showing up for those meetings, pointed at the writer's empty seat, and said: 'Please get that chair out of here.' Two weeks later, Sánchez Mazas was sacked, which (still according to legend) didn't seem to bother him too much. The causes of the dismissal were not clear. Some allege that Sánchez Mazas, whose position as Minister Without Portfolio lacked real content, was supremely bored by ministerial councils, because he was incapable of taking interest in bureaucratic and administrative affairs, which are what absorb the majority of a politician's time. Others maintain that it was Franco who was supremely bored by the erudite disquisitions on the most eccentric subjects (the causes of the defeat of the Persian fleet in the battle of Salamis, say; or the correct use of the jack plane) that Sánchez Mazas inflicted on him, and therefore decided to do without that inefficient, outlandish and untimely man of letters who played a virtually ornamental role in the government. There are even those who, whether out of innocence or bias, attribute Sánchez Mazas' idleness to disenchantment as a Falangist loyal to the authentic ideals of the party. All agree that he offered his resignation on several occasions, and that it was never accepted until his repeated absences from ministerial meetings, always justified by exotic excuses, made it a *fait accompli*. No matter which way you look at it, the legend is flattering to Sánchez Mazas, since it contributed to creating his image as an upright man, reluctant for the trappings of power. It is, most likely, false.

The journalist Carlos Sentís, who was his personal secretary during that period, maintains that the writer stopped attending the ministerial councils simply because he stopped being summoned to them. According to Sentís, certain inconvenient or extemporaneous declarations concerning the Gibraltar problem, along with the ill will the then all-powerful Serrano Súñer bore him, provoked his fall from grace. This version of events is reliable, to my mind, not only because Sentís was the person closest to Sánchez Mazas in the single year he lasted in the ministry, but also because it seems reasonable that Serrano Súñer would see in the tactlessness of Sánchez Mazas – who had conspired against him more than once to gain Franco's favour, just as he had in years gone by against Giménez Caballero to gain that of José Antonio – a perfect excuse to free himself of someone who, in his position as most senior 'old shirt', could represent a threat to his authority and erode his ascendancy over the orthodox Falangists and the Caudillo himself. Sentís claims that, as a result of his dismissal, Sánchez Mazas was confined for months in his house in the suburb of Viso – a cottage on Serrano Street he'd bought years before with his friend the Communist José Bergamín and which still belongs to the family – and deprived of his ministerial salary. His economic situation was getting ever more desperate, and in December, when they lifted the house arrest without any explanation, he decided to travel to Italy to ask for help from his wife's family. On his way he stayed at Sentís' house in Barcelona. Sentís doesn't retain an exact memory of those days, nor of Sánchez Mazas' state of mind, but he does recall that on Christmas day, just after the family celebrations, the writer received a providential telephone call from a relative, telling him that his aunt Julia Sánchez had just died and left him in her will a vast fortune including a mansion and several estates in Coria, in the province of Cáceres.

'You used to be a writer and a politician, Rafael,' Agustín de Foxá said to him around this time. 'Now you're just a millionaire.' Foxá was a writer and a politician and a millionaire, and one of the few friends Sánchez Mazas didn't end up losing over time. He was also a clever man, and as so often happens with clever men, he was often right. It's true that, after receiving his aunt's inheritance, Sánchez Mazas held various political posts – from member of the Leadership Council of the Falange through to Deputy Member of Parliament, by way of President of the Patrons' Association of the Prado Museum – but it's also true they were always secondary or decorative and barely took up his time and that from the middle of the forties he began to give them up as if shedding an annoying burden, and little by little, as time went by, he disappeared from public life. This does not mean, however, that Sánchez Mazas in the forties and fifties was a kind of silent opponent to Franco's government; he undoubtedly scorned the intellectual shoddiness and the mediocrity the regime had imposed on Spanish life, but he didn't feel uncomfortable in it, nor did he hesitate to proffer in public the most embarrassing dithyrambs to the tyrant and even, if it came to that, to his wife – though in private he flayed them for their stupidity and bad taste – and nor, of course, did he lament having contributed with all his might to inciting a war which razed a legitimate republic and failed to replace it with the terrible regime of poets and renaissance *condottieri* he'd dreamt of, but rather with a simple government of rogues, rustics and sanctimonious goody-goodies. 'I neither regret nor forget,' he famously wrote, by hand, in the full page frontispiece of *Foundation, Brotherhood and Destiny*, a book where he reprinted some of his bellicose articles of Falangist doctrine that in the thirties he'd published in *Arriba* and *F.E.* The phrase is from the spring of 1957; the date compels reflection. Madrid was then still in the grip of the backlash after the first great internal crisis of Francoism, stemming from an alliance, unexpected but in fact inevitable, between two groups Sánchez Mazas knew very well, because he lived with them on a daily basis. On one side, the young left-wing intelligentsia, an important part of which had arisen from the disillusioned ranks of the Falange itself and was made up of rebellious scions of notorious families of the regime, among them two of Sánchez Mazas' sons: Miguel, the first-born, one of the ring-leaders of the student rebellion of 1956 – who in February of that year was jailed and shortly afterwards left to a long exile – and Rafael, Sánchez Mazas' favourite, who had just published *El Jarama*, the novel in which the aesthetics and intellectual restlessness of those dissident youths came together; on the other side, a few 'old shirts' – among whom, in the front line, was Dionisio Ridruejo, an old friend of Sánchez Mazas, who had been arrested along with his son Miguel, and other student leaders from the anti-Franco outcry of the previous year, and in that same year, 1957, founded the social-democratic Social Party of Democratic Action – old Falangists from the early days who had perhaps not forgotten their political past, but who doubtless did regret it and were even undertaking, with more or less determination or courage, to combat the regime they had helped to bring about. I neither regret nor forget. Since emphatic loyalty so often denounces the traitor, there are some who suspect that if Sánchez Mazas wrote such a thing at such a time, it was precisely because, like some of his José Antonian comrades, he did regret – or at least partially regretted, and was trying to forget – or at least he was trying to partially forget. The conjecture is attractive, but false; in every case, apart from the secret disdain with which he contemplated the regime, not a single particular of his biography endorses it. 'If there's one thing I hate the Communists for, Your Excellency,' Foxá once said to Franco, 'it's for obliging me to join the Falange.' Sánchez Mazas would never have said such a thing –

too irreverent, too ironic – and much less in the presence of the General, but it undoubtedly goes for him too. Perhaps Sánchez Mazas was never more than a false Falangist, or else a Falangist who was only one because he felt obliged to be one – if all Falangists weren't false and obligatory ones, deep down never entirely believing that their ideology was anything other than a desperate measure in confusing times, an instrument destined to succeed in changing something in order that nothing change; I mean, had it not been because, like many of his comrades, he felt a real threat looming over his loved ones' sleep of bourgeois beatitude, Sánchez Mazas would never have stooped to getting involved in politics, nor would he have applied himself to forging the blazing rhetoric of the clash needed to inflame to victory the squad of soldiers charged with saving civilization. Sánchez Mazas identified civilization with the securities, privileges and hierarchies of his own people and the Falange with Spengler's squad of soldiers; but he also felt pride in having formed part of that squad and, perhaps, the right to rest after having restored hierarchies, securities and privileges. That's why it's doubtful he would have wanted to forget anything, and certain that he regretted nothing.

So, strictly speaking, it cannot be claimed that Sánchez Mazas was a politician during the post-war period; it would seem more contentious to maintain, as does clever Foxá, that nor was he a writer. Because it's true that in these years, as the political activity decreased, the literary increased: in the two decades following the war, novels, short stories, essays and theatre adaptations came out under his name, as well as innumerable articles appearing in *Arriba*, *La Tarde*, and *ABC*. Some of these articles are exceptional, finely crafted verbal jewels, and certain books he published then, like *The New Life of Pedrito de Andía*

(1951) and *The Waters of Arbeloa and Other Matters* (1956), figure among the best of his oeuvre. And yet it is also true that, although between the mid-forties and the mid-fifties he occupied a pre-eminent place in Spanish literature, he never bothered about having a literary career (an effort, like that of a political career, he always thought beneath the dignity of a gentleman), and as time went on he practised, with increasing skill, the subtle art of concealment, to the point where, for five years starting in 1955, he signed his *ABC* articles with three enigmatic asterisks. As to the rest, his social life was confined to assiduously keeping up with the few friends who, like Ignacio Agustí or Mariano Gómez Santos, had managed to survive the excesses of his character and, from the beginning of the fifties, the very occasional visit to the literary circle that César González-Ruano brought together at the Café Comercial at the Glorieta de Bilbao in Madrid. González-Ruano, who knew him well, at that time saw Sánchez Mazas 'as a great amateur, like a senior gentleman of letters, like a great, unmatched Señor who hadn't ever needed to make a profession of his vocations, but rather wrote verse and prose exercises during his vacations'.

In other words, Foxá was probably right after all: from the end of the war until his death, perhaps Sánchez Mazas was not essentially anything except a millionaire. A millionaire without many millions, languid and a bit decadent, given over to slightly extravagant passions – clocks, botany, magic, astrology – and the no less extravagant passion for literature. He divided his time between the mansion in Coria, where he spent long spells of *vie en château*, the Hotel Velásquez in Madrid, and the cottage in the suburb Viso, surrounded by cats, Italian flagstones, travel books, Spanish paintings and French engravings, with a big drawing room dominated by a fireplace, and a garden full of rose-bushes. He'd get up about midday and, after lunch, write until supper time; nights, which often stretched till dawn, he spent reading. He left the house very rarely; he smoked a lot. Probably by then he no longer believed in anything. Probably in his heart, never in his life had he truly believed in anything, and least of all, in what he'd defended or preached. He practised politics, but deep down always scorned them. He exalted time-honoured values – loyalty, courage – but practised treachery and cowardice, and contributed more than most to the brutal-ization the Falange's rhetoric inflicted on these values; he also exalted old institutions – the monarchy, the family, religion, the fatherland – but didn't lift a finger to bring a king to Spain, ignored his family, often living apart from them, would have exchanged all of Catholicism for a single canto of the *Divine Comedy* and as for the fatherland, well, no one knows what the fatherland is, or maybe it's simply an excuse for venality or sloth. Those who had dealings with him in his later years recall that he often remembered the vicissitudes of the war and the firing squad at Collell. 'It's incredible how much one learned in those few seconds of the execution,' he told a journalist in 1959, to whom, nevertheless, he did not reveal the learning he'd gained from the imminence of death. Perhaps he was no more than a survivor, and that's why at the end of his life he liked to imagine himself as a failed, autumnal gentleman, like someone who, having been capable of great things, had done almost nothing. 'I have but only in the most mediocre way measured up to the hope placed in me and help given me,' he confessed around this time to González-Ruano, and years before a character in *The New Life of Pedro de Andía* seems to speak for Sánchez Mazas when he proclaims from his deathbed: 'I've never been able to finish anything in this life.' In fact, it was in this way, melancholic, defeated and futureless, that he liked to portray himself from very early on. In July 1913, in Bilbao, barely nineteen years of age, Sánchez Mazas wrote, with the title 'Under an Ancient Sun', three sonnets, the last of which goes like this:

> In my twilight years as an old libertine
> and old courtly poet
> I'd spend the evenings, in contest
> with a devout Theatine Padre.
>
> Increasingly gouty and ever more Catholic,
> in the manner of an antiquated gentleman,
> my impertinent and haughty genius
> turning brittle and melancholic.
>
> And finding to end the story
> Masses and debts in my will,
> they'll give me a charity funeral.
>
> And fate in its final insult
> would wreathe its immortal laurels on me
> for a Moral Epistle to Fabius!*

* En mi ocaso de viejo libertino/ y de viejo poeta cortesano/ pasaría las tardes, mano a mano,/ con un beato padre teatino./ Cada vez más gotoso y más católico,/ como es guisa de rancio caballero,/ mi genio impertinente y altanero/ tornárse vidrioso y melancólico./ Y como hallasen para fin de cuento/ misas y deudas en mi testamento,/ de limosna me harían funerales./ Y la fortuna en su postrer agravio/ ciñérame sus lauros inmortales/ ¡por una Epístola moral a Fabio!

I don't know if at the end of his days, fifty years after writing those words, Sánchez Mazas was an old libertine, but there's no doubt he was an old courtly poet. He was still Catholic, although only outwardly, and also an antiquated gentleman. He always had an impertinent, haughty, brittle and melancholic genius. He died one October night in 1966, of pulmonary emphysema; few people attended his funeral. He left little money and not much property. He was a writer who didn't fulfil his promise and for that reason – and perhaps also because he was not worthy of it – did not write a *Moral Epistle to Fabius*. He was the best of the Falangist writers, leaving a handful of good poems and a handful of good prose pieces, which is much more than almost any writer can aspire to leave, but he left much less than his talent demanded, and his talent was always superior to his work. Andrés Trapiello says that, like so many Falangist writers, Sánchez Mazas won the war and lost the history of literature. The phrase is brilliant and, true in part – or at least it was, because for a while Sánchez Mazas paid for his brutal responsibility in a brutal war with oblivion – but it is also true that, having won the war, perhaps Sánchez Mazas lost himself as a writer. He was a romantic after all, would he not have judged deep down all victory to be contaminated by unworthiness, and the first thing he noticed upon arriving in paradise – albeit that illusory bourgeois paradise of leisure, chintz and slippers that, like a needy travesty of old privileges, hierarchies and securities, he constructed in his last years – was that he could live there, but not write, because writing and plenitude are incompatible. Few people remember him today, and perhaps that's what he deserves. There's a street named after him in Bilbao.

Part Three

RENDEZVOUS IN STOCKTON

I FINISHED WRITING *Soldiers of Salamis* long before the leave
of absence they'd given me from the newspaper ran out.
Conchi and I had dinner together two or three times a week,
but otherwise in all that time I hardly saw anyone, since I
spent day and night shut up in my room in front of the
computer. I wrote obsessively, with a drive and tenacity I
didn't know I possessed; also without being too sure of my
purpose. This entailed writing a sort of biography of Sánchez
Mazas which, focusing on an apparently anecdotal but perhaps
essential episode in his life – his botched execution at Collell –
would propose an interpretation of his character and, by
extension, of the nature of Falangism; or more precisely,
of the motives that induced the handful of cultivated and
refined men who founded the Falange to pitch the country
into a furious bloodbath. Naturally, I assumed that as the book
progressed, this plan would change, because books always end
up taking on a life of their own, and because a person doesn't
write about what he wants to write about but what he's
capable of writing about. I also assumed that, although
everything I'd found out about Sánchez Mazas over time
was going to form the nucleus of my book, which would allow
me to feel secure, a moment would arrive when I'd have to

dispense with those training wheels, because – if what he writes is going to have real interest – a writer never writes about what he knows, but precisely about what he does not know.

Neither of the two speculations were wrong, but by the middle of February, a month before my leave of absence was up, the book was finished. I read it euphorically; I reread it. At the second rereading my euphoria gave way to disappointment: the book wasn't bad, but insufficient, like a mechanism that was whole, yet incapable of performing the function for which it had been devised because it was missing a part. The worst of it was I didn't know what part it was. I revised the book thoroughly, I rewrote the beginning and the conclusion, I rewrote several episodes, I rearranged the order of others. The part, however, did not appear; the book remained hamstrung.

I gave up. The day I made the decision I went out for dinner with Conchi, who must have noticed I wasn't myself, because she asked me what was wrong. I didn't feel like talking about it (really, I didn't feel like talking at all, or even like going out for dinner), but I ended up explaining it to her.

'Shit!' said Conchi. 'Didn't I tell you not to write about a fascist? Those people fuck up everything they touch. What you have to do is forget all about that book and start another one. How about one on García Lorca?'

I spent the next two weeks sitting in an armchair in front of the television without turning it on. As far as I remember, I didn't think about anything, not even about my father, not even my ex-wife. Conchi visited me daily; she cleaned up the house a little, made me something to eat and once I'd gone to bed, she left. I didn't cry too much, but I couldn't help it each night when, at about ten o'clock, Conchi switched on the television to see herself dressed up as a fortune-teller on the local channel and then discuss her performance.

It was also Conchi who convinced me that, although my leave hadn't run out and I wasn't completely recovered, I should go back to work at the paper. Perhaps because I'd spent less time away than last time, or because my expression and appearance invited more pity than sarcasm, coming back empty-handed was less humiliating on this occasion, and there were no ironic comments from the editorial staff and no one asked me anything, not even the publisher; in fact, not only didn't he make me bring him coffee from the bar on the corner (an activity for which I'd come prepared), but he didn't even punish me with any other menial task. On the contrary, as if guessing I needed a bit of fresh air, he suggested I leave the culture section and instead conduct an almost daily series of interviews with people of some prominence who, not having been born in the province, had made it their home. That was how I ended up spending several months interviewing businessmen, athletes, poets, politicians, diplomats, ambulance chasers and idlers.

One of my first interviewees was Roberto Bolaño. Bolaño, who was a writer and from Chile, had been living for ages in Blanes, a coastal town on the border between the provinces of Barcelona and Gerona. He was forty-seven years old, with a good number of books behind him and that unmistakable air of a hippy peddler that afflicted so many Latin-Americans of his generation exiled in Europe. When I went to see him he'd just won a considerable literary prize and was living with his wife and son in Carrer Ample, a street in the centre of Blanes where he'd bought a modernist apartment with the prize money. He opened the door to me there that morning, and we hadn't even exchanged the customary greetings when he sprang on me:

'Hey, you're not the Javier Cercas of *The Motive* and *The Tenant*, are you?'

The Motive and *The Tenant* were the titles of the only two books I'd published, more than ten years before, without anyone except the odd friend from back then noticing. Bewildered or incredulous, I nodded.

'I know them,' he said. 'I think I even bought them.'

'Oh, so you were the one, were you?'

He ignored the joke.

'Hang on a second.'

He disappeared down a hallway and came back a little while later.

'Here they are,' he said, brandishing my books triumphantly.

I flipped through the two copies, saw they were worn. Almost sadly, I remarked:

'You read them.'

'Of course,' Bolaño sort of smiled; he almost never smiled but he never quite seemed to be entirely serious either. 'I read everything, even bits of paper I find blowing down the street.'

This time it was me who smiled.

'I wrote them ages ago.'

'You don't have to apologize,' he said. 'I liked them, or at least I remember liking them.'

I thought he was mocking me; I raised my gaze from the

books and looked him in the eye: he wasn't mocking. I heard myself ask:

'Really?'

Bolaño lit a cigarette and seemed to think it over for a moment.

'I don't remember the first one too well,' he finally admitted. 'But I think there was a really good story about a son of a bitch who persuades some poor guy to commit a crime so he can finish his novel, right?' Without giving me time to agree, he added: 'As for *The Tenant*, I thought it was a delightful little novel.'

Bolaño pronounced this judgement with such a mixture of ease and conviction that I suddenly knew those few bits of praise my books had received were products of courtesy or pity. I was speechless, and felt an enormous urge to hug that softly-spoken, curly-haired, scruffy, unshaven Chilean I'd only just met.

'Well,' I said. 'Shall we start the interview?'

We went to a bar by the port, between the market-place and the breakwater, and sat down by a large window from which we could make out, through the golden chilly morning air, the whole of Blanes bay, majestically criss-crossed by seagulls, with the dock in the foreground, its idle fishing boats, and in the background the Palomera promontory, marking the geographic border of the Costa Brava. Bolaño ordered tea and toast; I ordered coffee and water. We talked. Bolaño told me things were going well for him now, because his books were starting to bring in money, but for the last twenty years he'd been as poor as a church mouse. He'd quit school when he was practically still a kid; he'd had all kinds of odd jobs (though he'd never done any serious work other than writing); he'd been a revolutionary in Allende's Chile and in Pinochet's he'd been in prison; he'd lived in Mexico and France; he'd travelled all over the world. Years ago he'd undergone some very complicated surgery, and since then he lived the life of an ascetic in Blanes, with no other vice than writing, and seeing no one but his family. By chance, the day I interviewed Bolaño, General Pinochet had just returned to Chile to a hero's welcome from his supporters, after spending two years in England waiting to be extradited to Spain and tried for his crimes. We talked about Pinochet's return, about Pinochet's dictatorship, about Chile. Naturally, I asked him what it'd been like to live through Pinochet's coup and the fall of Allende. Naturally, he regarded me with an expression of utter boredom; then he said:

'Like a Marx Brothers' movie, but with corpses. Unimaginable pandemonium.' He blew a little on his tea, took a sip and put the cup back down on the saucer. 'Look, I'll tell you the truth. For years I spat on Allende's name every chance I got, I thought it was all his fault, for not giving us weapons. Now I kick myself for having said that about Allende. Fuck, the bastard thought about us as if we were his kids, you know? He didn't want them to kill us. And if he'd let us have those guns we would have died like flies. So,' he finished, picking up his cup again, 'I think Allende was a hero.'

'And what's a hero?'

The question seemed to surprise him, as if he'd never asked himself, or as if he'd been asking himself forever; his cup in mid-air, he looked me fleetingly in the eye, then turned his gaze back out over the bay and thought for a moment; then he shrugged his shoulders.

'I don't know,' he said. 'Someone who considers himself a hero and gets it right. Or someone who has courage and an instinct for virtue, and therefore never makes a mistake, or at least doesn't make a mistake the one time when it matters, and therefore can't *not* be a hero. Or someone, like Allende, who understands that a hero isn't the one who kills, but the one who doesn't kill or who lets himself get killed. I don't know. What's a hero to you?'

By then it had been almost a month since I'd thought about *Soldiers of Salamis*, yet at that moment I couldn't help but remember Sánchez Mazas, who never killed anyone and at some point, before reality showed him he lacked courage and an instinct for virtue, perhaps considered himself a hero. I said:

'I don't know. John Le Carré says one must think like a hero to behave like a decent human being.'

'Yeah, but a decent human being isn't the same as a hero,' Bolaño shot back. 'There're lots of decent people: they're the ones who know enough to say no in time; heroes, on the other hand, are few and far between. Actually, I think there's almost always something blind, irrational, instinctive in a hero's behaviour, something that's in their nature and inescapable. Also, you can be a decent person for a whole lifetime, but you can't be awe-inspiring without a break, and that's why a hero is only a hero exceptionally, once, or at most, during a spell of insanity or inspiration. There's Allende, speaking on Radio Magallanes, lying on the floor in a corner of La Moneda, with a machine gun in one hand and microphone in the other, talking as if he were drunk or as if he were already dead, not really knowing what he's saying and saying the purest, most noble words I've ever heard . . . I just remembered another story. It happened in Madrid a while back, I read it in the paper. A young guy was walking down a street in the city centre and suddenly saw a house enveloped in flames. Without a word to anyone he rushed into the house and came out with a woman in his arms. He went back in and this time brought a man out. Then he went in again and brought out another woman. By this time the fire had reached such proportions that not even the firemen would dare enter the house, it was suicide; but the guy must've known there was someone still inside, because he went back in. And, of course, he never came out.' Bolaño halted, pushed his glasses up with his index finger so the frame brushed his eyebrows. 'Brutal, isn't it? Still, I'm not sure that guy was acting out of compassion, or some sort of benevolence; I think he acted out of a kind of instinct, a blind instinct that overcame him, took him over, acted for him. More than likely the guy was a decent person, I'm not saying he wasn't; but he might not have been. Fuck, Javier, he didn't need to be: the bastard was a hero.'

Bolaño and I spent the rest of the morning talking about his books, the authors he liked – who were many – and the ones he despised – more still. Bolaño talked about them with a strange, icy passion, which fascinated me at first and then made me feel uncomfortable. I cut the interview short. When we were about to say goodbye, on the seaside promenade, he invited me to come and have lunch at his house, with his wife and son. I lied: I said I couldn't, because they were expecting me back at the paper. Then he invited me to come and see him some time. I lied again: I said I would very soon.

A week later, when the interview was published, Bolaño phoned me at the newspaper office. He said he'd liked it a lot. He asked:

'Are you sure I said all that about heroes?'

'Word for word,' I answered, suddenly suspicious, thinking the initial praise was just a preamble to the reproaches, and that Bolaño was one of those loquacious interviewees who attribute all their verbal indiscretions to journalists' spite, negligence or frivolity. 'I've got it on tape.'

'No shit! Well, it sounded pretty good!' he reassured me. 'But I called you about something else. I'm going to be in Gerona tomorrow, I have to renew my residency permit – a fucking nuisance, but it won't take me very long. Do you want to meet for lunch?'

I hadn't expected the call or the suggestion and, perhaps because it seemed easier to accept than make up an excuse, I accepted, and the next day, when I arrived at the Bistrot, Bolaño was already sitting at a table with a Diet Coke in hand.

'It's been at least twenty years since I've been here,' remarked Bolaño, who on the phone the previous day had told me that, when he used to live in the city, his place was near the Bistrot. 'This has changed a fuck of a lot.'

After having ordered (steak and salad for him; steamed mussels and rabbit for me), Bolaño repeated his praise for my interview, he talked about Capote and Mailer, then asked me suddenly if I was writing anything. Since nothing annoys a writer who doesn't write as much as being asked what he's writing, I answered, slightly irritated:

145

'No.' And because I figured for Bolaño, like for everyone, writing for a newspaper wasn't really writing, I added: 'I don't write novels any more.' I thought of Conchi and said: 'I've discovered I have no imagination.'

'To write novels you don't need an imagination,' Bolaño said. 'Just a memory. Novels are written by combining recollections.'

'Then I've run out of memories.' Trying to be witty I explained: 'I'm a journalist now: a man of action.'

'Well, that's a shame,' said Bolaño, 'a man of action is a frustrated writer. If Don Quixote had written one single book of chivalry he never would have been Don Quixote, and if I hadn't learned how to write I'd be firing away with the FARC right now. Besides, a real writer never stops being a writer. Even if they don't write.'

'What makes you think I'm a real writer?'

'You wrote two real books.'

'Juvenilia.'

'The newspaper doesn't count?'

'It counts. But I don't write for pleasure there: just to make a living. Besides, a journalist isn't the same thing as a writer.'

'You're right there,' he conceded. 'A good journalist is always a good writer, but a good writer is almost never a good journalist.'

I laughed.

'Dazzling, but false,' I said.

While we ate, Bolaño told me about when he'd lived in Gerona; he described minutely an interminable February night in one of the city's hospitals, the Josep Trueta. That morning they'd diagnosed him with pancreatitis and when the doctor finally appeared in his room, he asked him, knowing what the answer would be, if he was going to die; the doctor stroked his arm and told him no in the voice they always reserve for lies. Before falling asleep that night, Bolaño felt profoundly sad, not because he knew he was going to die, but for all the books he'd planned to write and would now never write, for all his dead friends, all the young Latin Americans of his generation – soldiers killed in wars already lost – he'd always dreamt of resuscitating in his novels and who'd now stay dead forever, just like him, as if he'd never existed; then he fell asleep and during the night dreamt he was in a ring fighting a sumo wrestler, a gigantic and smiling Oriental against whom he could do nothing and against whom, nevertheless, he kept fighting all night long until he woke up and knew, before anyone told him, with a superhuman joy he'd never felt since, that he wasn't going to die.

'But sometimes I think I still haven't woken up,' Bolaño said wiping his mouth with his serviette. 'Sometimes I think I'm still in that bed in the Trueta, fighting that sumo wrestler, and everything that's happened over these years (my son and my wife and the novels I've written and my dead friends I've talked about) is what I've dreamed, and at some moment I'll wake up and I'll be on the canvas in the ring, murdered by a big fat Oriental guy who smiles just like death.'

After lunch Bolaño asked me to go for a walk with him around the city. I went with him: we walked through the old part of the city, down the Rambla, across the Plaza de Catalunya, through the market-place. At dusk we went to have a drink in the bar of the Hotel Carlemany, quite near the station, while Bolaño waited for his train. It was there, between cups of tea and gin and tonics, that he told me the story of Miralles. I don't remember why or how he got to it; I remember he talked with an unwavering enthusiasm, with a sort of jubilant seriousness, putting all his military and historical erudition at the service of the tale, which was overwhelming but not always precisely accurate, because later when I consulted several books on the military operations of the Civil War and the Second World War, I discovered that some of the dates and names and circumstances had been modified by his imagination or his memory. Yet for the most part, the tale not only seems true, but is also, in most of its details, verifiable.

Once the few facts and dates Bolaño had altered have been corrected, the story goes like this:

Bolaño met Miralles in the summer of 1978, in the Estrella de Mar campsite, in Castelldefells. The Estrella de Mar was a caravan site where a floating population, comprised basically of members of the European proletariat, would show up each summer: French, English, Dutch, Germans, the odd Spaniard. Bolaño remembered that, at least during the time he spent there, those people were very happy; he also remembered that he, too, was happy. He worked at the campsite for four summers, from 1978 to 1981, sometimes on weekends in the winters too; he worked as rubbish collector, night watchman, everything.

'It was my doctorate,' Bolaño assured me. 'I got to know such a range of human fauna. Actually, never in my life have I learned so many things, so quickly, as I did there.'

Miralles arrived every year at the beginning of August. Bolaño remembered him driving up with his caravan, with his exuberant greetings, his huge smile, his cap pulled down over

148

his brow and his enormous buddha's belly, registering at the office and setting up immediately at his assigned site. From that moment on Miralles never wore more than swimming trunks and a pair of flip-flops for the rest of the month and, since he walked around undressed all day, he attracted attention from the start because his body was a real compendium of scars. In fact, his whole left side, from his ankle all the way up to his eye, out of which he could still see, was one entire scar. Miralles was Catalan, from Barcelona or near Barcelona – Sabadell maybe, or Terrassa: in any case Bolaño remembered having heard him speak Catalan – but he'd been living in France for years and, according to Bolaño, he'd become completely French: he wielded a sharp sense of irony, ate and drank well and loved good wine. In the evenings he'd get together with his old campsite friends from every summer in the bar and Bolaño, as night watchman, would often join these sessions that went on far into the night; he saw Miralles get drunk on many occasions, but he never saw him turn aggressive or rowdy or sentimental. At the end of such nights he simply needed someone to take him back to his caravan, because he couldn't get there by himself. Bolaño helped him many times, and also sat up late with him in the bar, drinking on their own long after Miralles had outlasted all his mates, and it was during these interminable solitary nights (he never saw him talk about it in front of others) that he listened to him unfurl his war record – unfurl it without boasting, without pride, with the learned irony of an adoptive Frenchman, as if it didn't belong to him but to some other person, someone he barely knew but whom he vaguely respected. That's why Bolaño remembered his tale with absolute precision.

149

Miralles was recruited in the autumn of 1936, a few months after the beginning of the war in Spain and after he had just turned eighteen; at the beginning of 1937, after some hasty military training, he was placed in the First Mixed Brigade of the Army of the Republic, which was under the command of Enrique Líster. Líster, who'd been commander of the Antifascist Workers' Militias and of the Fifth Regiment, was already a living legend. The Fifth Regiment had just been disbanded, and the majority of Miralles' battalion comrades had fought in its ranks and had been decisive, a few months earlier in November, in stopping Franco's troops at the gates of Madrid. Before the war Miralles worked as an apprentice lathe operator; he knew nothing about politics: his parents were very poor and never discussed such things; nor did his friends. Nevertheless, as soon as he arrived at the front, he became a Communist: the fact that his comrades and commanders and Líster were Communists undoubtedly influenced his decision too; perhaps even more so did his immediate certainty that the Communists were the only ones who were really ready to stand firm and win the war.

'I guess he was a bit wild,' Bolaño remembered Miralles saying one night, talking about Líster, under whose orders he'd spent the entire war. 'But he loved his men and he was very brave, very Spanish. A guy with real guts.'

'A thoroughbred Spanish brute,' Bolaño quoted, without telling Miralles he was quoting César Vallejo, about whom he was writing a quirky novel at the time.

Miralles laughed.

'Exactly,' he agreed. 'Afterwards I read a lot about him, against him really. Most of it false, from what I know. I suppose he was wrong about a lot of things, but he got a lot of things right too, don't you think?'

In the early days of the war Miralles had been in sympathy with the anarchists, not so much for their chaotic ideas or for their urge to revolution, but more because they were the first to take to the streets and fight against fascism. Nevertheless, as the struggle advanced and the anarchists spread chaos in the rearguard, that sympathy disappeared: like all Communists – and undoubtedly this also helped push him towards them – Miralles understood that the first thing was to win the war, then there would be time for revolution. So, in the summer of 1937 when the 11th Division, to which he belonged, liquidated the Aragonese anarchist collectives on Líster's orders, Miralles considered the operation brutal, but not unjustified. Later he fought in Belchite, in Teruel, at the Ebro and, when the front collapsed, Miralles retreated with the army towards Catalonia and at the beginning of 1939 crossed the French border together with the other 450,000 Spaniards who did so in the final days of the war. On the other side was the Argelès concentration camp, which was really just a bare, immense beach surrounded by a double ring of barbed wire; there were no huts, and no protection from the savage February cold, and no sanitation, just a quagmire, where in subhuman conditions, with women and old folks and children sleeping on the sand dappled with snow and frost, and men wandering around, dumbfounded by the burden of desperation and the rancour of defeat, 80,000 Spanish fugitives waited for the hell to end.

'They called them concentration camps,' Miralles used to say. 'But they were nothing but death-traps.'

And so, a few weeks after arriving at Argelès, when the

enlistment flags of the French Foreign Legion appeared in the camp, Miralles signed up without a second thought. That was how he ended up in the Maghreb, some part of the Maghreb, maybe Tunisia or Algeria, Bolaño didn't quite remember. The beginning of the World War caught him out there. France fell into the hands of the Germans in June of 1940, and the majority of the French authorities in the Maghreb took the side of the puppet government at Vichy. But Leclerc, General Jacques Phillippe Leclerc, was also in the Maghreb. Leclerc refused to accept orders from Vichy and began to recruit as many people as he could, with the reckless idea of getting them to cross half of Africa under his command and reach some French overseas possession that accepted the authority of De Gaulle, who like him, though from London, had rebelled against Pétain in the name of Free France.

'Fuck, Javier!' Reclining in an armchair in the bar of the Carlemany, Bolaño looked at me mockingly or incredulous through the thick lenses of his glasses and smoke of his Ducados. 'Miralles spent his whole life cursing Leclerc, and also himself for having listened to Leclerc. Neither he nor any of the other outcasts Leclerc took for suckers had the slightest idea of where they were heading. It was a journey of several thousand kilometres across the desert, pure hell, and in much worse conditions than Miralles had left behind in Argelès and with hardly any provisions. Paris-Dakar was a joke, a fucking little Sunday stroll in comparison! It'd take real balls to do a thing like that!'

Nevertheless, there were Miralles and his bunch of deluded volunteers urgently recruited by Leclerc's ludicrous proselytism, who, after several months of suicidal countermarches through the desert, arrived in the province of Chad, in French Equatorial Africa, where they finally made contact with De Gaulle's people. A short time after getting to Chad, together with an English detachment from Cairo and in the company of five other men from the Foreign Legion under the command of Colonel D'Ornano, Commander-in-Chief of the French forces in Chad, Miralles took part in the attack on the Italian oasis of Murzuk, in south-western Libya. The six members of the French patrol were in theory volunteers; in reality Miralles would never have participated in that raid had it not been for the fact that, since no one in his company volunteered for it, they drew lots and Miralles ended up losing. Miralles' patrol was symbolic more than anything, because after the fall of France, it was the first time a French contingent took part in an act of war against the Axis powers.

'Just imagine, Javier,' said Bolaño, looking slightly perplexed, as if holding back laughter, and as if he himself were discovering the story (or the meaning of the story) as he told it. 'All of Europe dominated by the Nazis, and there in the back of beyond, without anyone knowing it, these four fucking Moors, a fucking black guy and this bastard of a Spaniard who made up D'Ornano's patrol raising the flag of freedom for the first time in months. Fucking incredible! And there's Miralles, shafted and shit out of luck and probably with no idea what he's doing there. But there he was.'

Colonel D'Ornano fell at Murzuk. His post in command of the forces in Chad was covered by Leclerc, who, spurred on by the success at Murzuk, immediately launched an attack against the oasis of Koufra – the most important of the Libyan desert, and also in Italian hands – with a handful of volunteers from the Foreign Legion and a handful of natives, with very few weapons and very little transport, and on 1 March 1941, after another march of more than a thousand kilometres across the desert, Leclerc and his men took Koufra. And there, naturally, was Miralles. Back in Chad, Miralles enjoyed his first weeks of rest in years, and at some point various deceptive signs led him to imagine that, after the heroic achievements of Murzuk and Koufra, the war was going to keep well away from him and his comrades for some time. That was when Leclerc had his second brilliant idea in a very short time. Convinced, and rightly so, that the war was at stake in North Africa, where Montgomery's Eighth Army was fighting against the German Afrika-Korps, he decided to try to join the English troops, carrying out the reverse of the march – from the Maghreb to Chad – that they'd carried out months earlier. Other Allied units executed the same or a similar operation at the time, but Leclerc was entirely lacking any infrastructure, so Miralles and the 3,200 men he'd managed to gather by then had to cross the thousands of kilometres of merciless desert that separated them from Tripoli once again, by foot, and in even more precarious conditions than the first time, arriving finally in January 1943, just when Rommel's troops had been expelled from the city by Montgomery's Eighth Army. Leclerc's column spent the rest of the African campaign with that corps, so Miralles fought the Germans in the offensive against the Mareth line, and later the Italians in Gabes and Sfax.

Once the African campaign was over, Leclerc's column, integrated into the organizational structure of the Allied Army, became motorized, turning into the 2nd Armoured

Division and, after being sent to England for training in the handling of American tanks, on 1 August 1944, almost two months after D-Day, Miralles disembarked on Utah beach in Normandy, operating with Hislip's XV Army Corps. Leclerc's column left immediately for the front, and during the twenty-three days the French campaign lasted for Miralles, he didn't stop fighting for an instant, especially in the region of Sarthe and in the battles that preceded the definitive isolation of the Falaise pocket. Because at that time Leclerc's was a very special unit: not only was it the only French division to fight on French soil (full though it was of Africans and Spanish veterans of the Civil War, which the name of their tanks proclaimed: Guadalajara, Zaragoza, Belchite), but it was also a division made up exclusively of volunteers, so that it couldn't count on fresh relief troops like a normal division could and when a soldier fell, his post was left empty until another volunteer came to fill it. This explains how, although no sensible commander keeps a soldier in the front line of combat for more than four or five months at a time, because the tension of the front is unbearable, when Miralles and his comrades from the Civil War stepped on the beaches of Normandy, they'd been fighting non-stop for more than seven years.

But the war still hadn't ended for them. Leclerc's column was the first Allied contingent to enter Paris; Miralles did so by the Porte-de-Gentilly on the night of 24 August, barely an hour after the first French detachment under the command of Captain Dronne. Fifteen days had not yet passed when Leclerc's men, now integrated into de Lattre de Tassigny's Third French Army, entered combat again. The following weeks gave them not a moment's respite: they charged the Sigfried line, penetrated into Germany, and got as far as Austria. There Miralles' military adventure ended. There, on a windy winter morning he'd never forget, Miralles (or someone next to Miralles) stepped on a mine.

'He was blown to shreds,' said Bolaño, after pausing to finish his tea, which had gone cold in the cup. 'The war in Europe was just about to end and, after eight years of combat, Miralles had seen loads of people die around him, friends and comrades from Spain, Africa, France, everywhere. His turn had come . . .' Bolaño thumped his fist down on the arm of the chair. 'His turn had come, but the bastard didn't die. They took him to the rearguard all blown to shit and put him back together again as best they could. Incredibly, he survived. And slightly over a year later, there's Miralles converted into a French citizen and with a pension for life.'

When the war ended and he had recovered from his injuries, Miralles went to live in Dijon, or some place around Dijon, Bolaño didn't quite remember exactly. On more than one occasion he'd asked Miralles why he'd settled there, and sometimes he answered that he'd settled there just as he might have settled anywhere, and other times he said he'd settled there because during the war he'd promised himself that, if he managed to survive, he was going to spend the rest of his life drinking fine wine, 'and so far I've kept the faith', he'd add, patting his bare and happy buddha's belly. When he used to see Miralles, Bolaño thought that neither of those answers were true; now he thought maybe they both were. The fact is that Miralles married in Dijon (or around Dijon) and in Dijon (or around Dijon) he'd had a daughter. Her name was María.

Bolaño met her at the campsite; at the beginning she'd come with her father every summer: he remembered an elegant, serious and strong-willed girl, 'thoroughly French', although she always spoke a Spanish dappled with guttural 'r's to her father. Bolaño also recalled that Miralles, who'd become a widower shortly after she was born, was totally soft on her: it was María who ran the house, María who gave orders which Miralles obeyed with the modest humility of a veteran used to obeying orders, and who, when the conversation went on too long at the camp bar and the wine started to make Miralles' mouth pasty and tangle up his sentences, took him by the arm and led him to the caravan, docile and stumbling, with the blurred gaze of a drinker and guilty smile of a proud father. María, however, only came for a short time, no more than two years (two of the four that Bolaño worked at the campsite), and then Miralles started to come to Estrella de Mar on his own. It was then that Bolaño really got to know him; that was also when Miralles started sleeping with Luz. Luz was a prostitute who worked the campsite for a few summers. Bolaño remembered her well: dark and chubby and quite young and good-looking, with a natural generosity and imperturbable common sense; perhaps she only occasionally worked as a hooker, Bolaño speculated.

'Miralles fell for Luz really hard,' he added. 'The poor bastard would get so sad and drink himself into a stupor when she wasn't around.'

Bolaño then remembered that one night of the last summer he spent with Miralles, while he was doing his first round, in the early hours of the morning, he heard some very soft music coming from the edge of the campsite, just beside the fence that separated it from a pinewood. More out of curiosity than to demand they turn off the music – it was playing so softly that it couldn't have disturbed anybody's sleep – he approached discreetly and saw a couple dancing in each other's arms beneath the awning of a caravan. He recognized the caravan as that of Miralles; the couple as Miralles and Luz; the music, as a very sad and very old paso doble (or that's what it seemed to Bolaño) that he'd often heard Miralles hum under his breath. Before they could sense his presence, Bolaño hid behind a caravan and spent several minutes watching them. They were dancing very close, very seriously, in silence, barefoot on the grass, wrapped in the unreal light of the moon and an old butane lantern, and Bolaño was struck most of all by the contrast between the solemnity of their movements and their attire – Miralles in his swimming trunks, as ever, old and potbellied, but marking the steps with the sure elegance of a dancehall regular, leading Luz, who perhaps because she was wearing a white blouse that reached her knees and allowed glimpses of her naked body, seemed to float like a phantom in the cool night air. Bolaño said that at that moment, spying from behind a trailer on that old veteran of all the wars, with his body sewn up by scars and his soul bared to a sometime hooker who didn't know how to dance a paso doble, he felt a strange emotion, like a reflection of that emotion, perhaps a deceptive one, and as the couple turned, he thought he saw a sparkle in Miralles' eyes, as if just then he'd begun to cry or tried in vain to hold back his tears or maybe he'd been crying for a long time, and then Bolaño realized or imagined that his presence there was somehow obscene, that he was stealing that scene from someone and that he had to leave, and he also realized, vaguely, that his time at the campsite had come to an end, because he'd learned all he could learn there. So he lit a cigarette, looked one last time at Luz and Miralles dancing under the awning, turned and continued on his round.

'At the end of that summer I said see you next year to Miralles as usual,' Bolaño said after a long silence, as if he were talking to himself, or rather to someone who was listening to him but who wasn't me. On the other side of the Carlemany's windows it was already night; facing me was Bolaño's cloudy, absent expression and a table with several empty glasses and an ashtray overflowing with stubbed out cigarette butts. We'd asked for the bill. 'But I knew I wouldn't go back to the campsite the following year. And I didn't go back. I never saw Miralles again.'

I insisted on accompanying Bolaño to the station and, while he was buying a pack of Ducados for the trip, I asked him whether in all these years he'd ever heard anything more about Miralles.

'Nothing,' he answered. 'I lost track of him, like so many people. Who knows where he is now. Maybe he still goes to the campsite; but I don't think so. He'd be over eighty, and I doubt very much if he'd be up to it. Maybe he still lives in Dijon. Or maybe he's dead, really I guess that's the most likely, no? Why do you ask?'

'No reason,' I said.

But it wasn't true. That afternoon, as I listened with growing interest to the exaggerated tale of Miralles, I thought that I'd soon be reading it in one of Bolaño's exaggerated books; but when I got home, after seeing my friend off and walking through the city lit by street lamps and shop windows, and perhaps carried away by the exaltation of the gin and tonics, I had already begun to hope that Bolaño wasn't ever going to write that story: I was going to write it. I kept going over the idea in my mind all evening. While I was making dinner, while I was eating, while I washed the dishes after dinner, while I drank a glass of milk watching the television but without seeing it, I imagined a beginning and an ending, organized episodes, invented characters, mentally wrote and rewrote many sentences. Lying in bed, wide awake in the dark (only the numbers on the digital alarm clock gave off a red glow in the thick darkness of the bedroom), my head was seething, and at some moment, inevitably, because age and failure impart prudence, I tried to rein in my enthusiasm by remembering my latest disaster. That was when I thought of it. I thought of Sánchez Mazas and the firing squad and that Miralles had been one of Líster's soldiers all through the war, that he'd been with him in Madrid, in Aragón, at the Ebro, in the retreat through Catalonia. Why not at Collell?, I thought. And at that moment, with the deceptive but overwhelming clarity of insomnia, like someone who finds, by unbelievable chance, having already given up the search (because a person never finds what he's searching for, but what reality delivers), the missing part to complete the mechanism that was otherwise whole yet incapable of performing the function for which it had been devised, I heard myself murmur, in the pitch-black silence of the bedroom: 'It's him.'

I jumped out of bed, and barefoot, in three strides, I was in the dining room; I picked up the telephone and dialled Bolaño's number. I was waiting for someone to answer when I saw the clock on the wall said three-thirty. I hesitated for a moment; then I hung up.

I think towards dawn I managed to get to sleep. Before nine I phoned Bolaño again. His wife answered; Bolaño was still in bed. I didn't manage to speak to him until twelve, from the office. Almost straight out I asked him if he intended to write about Miralles; he said no. Then I asked him if he'd ever heard Miralles mention the Sanctuary of Collell; Bolaño made me repeat the name.

'No,' he said at last. 'Not that I recall.'

'What about Rafael Sánchez Mazas?'

'The writer?'

'Yeah,' I said. 'Ferlosio's father. Do you know him?'

'I've read a couple of things of his, pretty good, I'd have to say. But why would Miralles mention him? We never talked about literature. And, anyway, what's this interrogation all about?'

I was about to avoid his question when I realized in time that only through Bolaño could I get to Miralles. Briefly, I explained.

'Fuck, Javier!' Bolaño exclaimed. 'You've got a hell of a novel there. I knew you were writing something.'

'I'm not writing.' Contradicting myself, I added, 'And it's not a novel. It's a story with real events and characters. A true tale.'

'Same difference,' replied Bolaño. 'All good tales are true tales, at least for those who read them, which is all that counts. Anyway, what I don't get is how you can be so sure that Miralles is the militiaman who saved Sánchez Mazas.'

'Who said I was? I'm not even sure he was at Collell. All I'm saying is that Miralles could have been there and, therefore, could have been the militiaman.'

'Could have been,' murmured Bolaño sceptically. 'But most probably wasn't. In any event –'

'In any event, it's a case of finding him and settling the matter,' I cut him off, guessing the way his sentence was going to end ('. . . if it's not him, you pretend it was him'). 'That's why I called you. The question is: have you any idea how to locate Miralles?'

Exhaling loudly, Bolaño reminded me that he hadn't seen Miralles for twenty years, and that he wasn't friends with anyone from back then, anyone who could – he stopped short and, offering no explanation, asked me to hang on a moment. I hung on. The moment got so long that I thought Bolaño must have forgotten I was waiting on the phone.

'You're in luck, you bastard,' I heard eventually. Then he read out a telephone number to me. 'That's Estrella de Mar. I'd completely forgotten I had it, but I've still got all my diaries from back then. Call and ask about Miralles.'

'What was his first name?'

'Antoni, I think. Or Antonio. I don't know. Everybody called him Miralles. Call and ask for him: in my day we kept a register with the names and addresses of all the people who stayed at the campsite. I'm sure they still do . . . That's if Estrella de Mar still exists, of course.'

I hung up. I picked the phone back up. I dialled the number Bolaño had given me. Estrella de Mar still existed, and had already opened its gates for the summer season. I asked the female voice that answered if a person called Antoni or Antonio Miralles was staying at the campsite; after a few seconds, during which I heard the distant typing of speedy fingers, she told me no. I explained the situation: I urgently needed the details of this person, who had been a regular client of Estrella de Mar twenty years earlier. The voice hardened: she assured me that it was not their custom to give out details of their clients and, while I heard the nervous typing start up again, she informed me that two years earlier they had computerized the campsite register, keeping only data relating to the last eight years. I insisted: I said that perhaps Miralles had been coming to the campsite till then. 'I assure you he hasn't,' said the girl. 'How?' said I. 'Because he's not in our archive. I've just checked. There are two Miralles, but neither of them is called Antonio. Or Antoni.' 'Are either of them called María?' 'No.'

That morning, extremely excited but exhausted, I told Conchi Miralles' story while we were having lunch at a self-service restaurant, explaining the error of perspective I'd committed when writing *Soldiers of Salamis* and assuring her that Miralles (or someone like Miralles) was exactly the part that was missing in order for the mechanism of the book to function. Conchi stopped eating, half closed her eyes and said, with resignation:

'About time Lucas took a shit.'

'Lucas? Who's Lucas?'

'Nobody,' said Conchi. 'A friend. He took a shit after he died and he died of not shitting.'

'Conchi, please, we're eating. Anyway, what's this Lucas got to do with Miralles?'

'Sometimes you remind me of Brains, honey,' Conchi sighed. 'If I didn't know you were an intellectual, I'd say you were stupid. Didn't I tell you at the start what you had to do was write about a Communist?'

'Conchi, I don't think you've really understood what —'

'Of course I understand!' she interrupted me. 'The amount of grief we would have saved if you'd listened to me in the first place! And, you know what I say?'

'What?' I said, slightly uneasily.

'We're going to come out with a fucking brilliant book!'

We clinked glasses, and for a moment I was tempted to stretch out my foot to see if Conchi had any panties on; for a moment I thought I was in love with her. Prudent and happy, I said:

'I haven't found Miralles yet.'

'We'll find him,' said Conchi, with absolute conviction. 'Where did you say Bolaño said he lived?'

'In Dijon,' I said. 'Or somewhere around there.'

'Well, that's where we'll have to start looking.'

That evening I called Telefónica's international directory enquiries. The operator told me that in the city of Dijon and in the whole of Department 21, to which Dijon belonged, there was no one called Antoni or Antonio Miralles. I then asked if there were a María Miralles; the operator said there was not. I asked if there were *any* Miralles, and was surprised to hear her say there were five: one in the city of Dijon and four in villages of the Department: one in Longuic, another in Marsannay, another in Nolay and another in Genlis. I asked her to give me their names and telephone numbers. 'Impossible,' she said. 'I can only give out one name and one number per call. You'd have to call back another four times for us to give you all of them.'

During the following days I phoned the Miralles who lived in Dijon (Laurent, he was called) and the other four, whose names were Laura, Danielle, Jean-Marie and Bienvenido. Two of them (Laurent and Danielle) were brother and sister, and all except Jean-Marie spoke correct (or broken) Castilian, since they came from Spanish families, but none of them were remotely related to Miralles, and none had ever heard of him.

I didn't give up. Perhaps driven by the blind faith Conchi had instilled in me, I phoned Bolaño. I brought him up to date with my investigation and asked him if he could think of any other trail I could follow up. Not a single one occurred to him.

'You'll have to make it up,' he said.

'Make what up?'

'The interview with Miralles. It's the only way you can finish the novel.'

It was at that moment I remembered the story from my first book that Bolaño had recalled in our first conversation, in which a man induces another to commit a crime so he can finish his novel, and I believed I understood two things. The first surprised me; the second did not. The first was that finishing the book mattered much less to me than being able to talk to Miralles; the second was that, contrary to what Bolaño had believed up till now (and contrary to what *I'd* believed when I wrote my first book), I wasn't a real writer, because if I were, talking to Miralles would have mattered much less than finishing the book. I decided not to remind Bolaño again that my book wasn't meant to be a novel, but a true tale, and that making up the interview with Miralles would amount to a betrayal of its nature, and sighed:

'Yeah.'

The answer was laconic, not affirmative; Bolaño didn't take it that way.

'It's the only way,' he repeated, sure he had convinced me. 'Besides, it's the best way. Reality always ends up betraying us; it's best not to give her the chance and get in there first. The real Miralles would only disappoint you. Better to make him up; the invented one will surely be more real than the real one. You're not going to find him. Who knows where he might be: dead, in a home, in his daughter's house. Forget him.'

'It's best we just forget about Miralles,' I told Conchi that night, having survived a terrifying trip to her house in Quart followed by a hurried tumble in the living room, under the devoted gaze of the Virgin of Guadalupe and the melancholic gaze of the copies of my two books that flanked her. 'Who knows where he might be: dead or in a home or in his daughter's house.'

'Have you looked for his daughter?'

'Yes. But I haven't found her.'

We stared at each other for a second – two – three. Then, without another word, I got up, went to the phone, dialled Telefónica's international directory enquiries. I told the operator (I think I recognized her voice; I think she recognized mine) that I was looking for a person who lived in an old people's home in Dijon and I asked her how many old people's homes there were in Dijon. 'Oh,' she said after a pause, 'loads.' 'How many's loads?' 'Thirty odd. Maybe forty.' 'Forty old people's homes!' I looked at Conchi who, sitting on the floor, and barely covered by her T-shirt, held back her laughter. 'Is there no one but old people in that city?' 'The computer doesn't specify whether they're old people's homes,' the operator clarified. 'It just says residential home.' 'And how many are there in the Department?' After another pause she replied: 'More than twice as many.' Slightly sarcastically she added: 'I can only give you one number per call. Should I start alphabetically?' I thought this was the end of my search; making sure Miralles didn't live at any of these eighty some residential homes could take me months and I could end up broke – not to mention that I didn't have the slightest reason to believe he did live in any of them, and even less that he was the soldier of Líster's I was looking for. I looked at Conchi, who looked back at me drumming her fingers impatiently on her bare knees; I looked at my books beside the Virgin of Guadalupe and – I don't know why – I thought of Daniel Angelats. Then, as if getting even with someone, I said: 'Yes. Alphabetically please.'

That was how a telephonic pilgrimage began, a pilgrimage that would last for a month of daily long-distance calls, first to the residential homes of the city of Dijon and then to those of the entire Department. The procedure was always the same. I called international directory inquiries, asked for the next name and number on the list (Abrioux, Bagatelle, Cellerier, Chambertin, Chanzy, Éperon, Fontainemont, Kellerman, Lyautey were the first lot), I called the home, asked the switchboard operator for Monsieur Miralles, they answered that there was no Monsieur Miralles there, I phoned international directory inquiries again, asked for another telephone number, and so on until I got tired of it; and the next day (or the one after, because sometimes I couldn't find the time or the will to go back into my obsessive roulette) took up the trail again. Conchi helped me, luckily: I now think that, if not for her, I would have abandoned the search early on. We called in our spare time, almost always secretly, me from the editorial offices, her from the television studio. Then, every night, we'd compare notes on the day, exchange the names of ruled out residential homes, and during those conversations I realized that for Conchi, the monotony of daily telephone calls in search of a man who we didn't even know was alive was an unexpected and exciting adventure; and as for me, at first infected by Conchi's investigative drive and straightforward conviction, I bent to the task enthusiastically, but after I'd surveyed the first thirty homes I began to suspect that I was doing it more out of inertia or stubbornness (or so as not to let Conchi down) than because I still held some hope of finding Miralles.

But one night the miracle happened. I'd finished writing a short article and we were putting the paper to bed when I started my round of calls by dialling the number of the Nimphéas Residential Home in Fontaine-Lès-Dijon, and, when I asked for Miralles, instead of the usual negative, the switchboard operator answered me with silence. I thought she'd hung up and I was about to do the same, routinely, when a masculine voice stopped me in my tracks.

'*Allô?*'

I repeated the question that I'd just asked the operator and that we'd spent more than ten days asking in an absurd tour of all the residential homes in Department 21.

'Miralles here,' said the man in Spanish: the surprise kept me from noticing that my rudimentary French had given me away. 'Who am I speaking to?'

'Antoni Miralles?' I managed to mumble.

'Antoni or Antonio, whatever,' he said. 'But call me Miralles; everybody calls me Miralles. Who am I speaking to?'

It strikes me as incredible now but, no doubt because deep down I never really thought I'd end up talking to Miralles, I hadn't thought through how I'd introduce myself to him.

'You don't know me, but I've been trying to track you down for ages,' I improvised, aware of a pulse in my throat and a tremor in my voice. To disguise them, I quickly told him my name and where I was calling from. Fortunately I added: 'I'm a friend of Roberto Bolaño's.'

'Roberto Bolaño?'

'Yes, from the Estrella de Mar campsite,' I explained. 'In Castelldefells. Many years ago you and he —'

'Of course!' I was grateful, rather than relieved, for the interruption. 'The caretaker! I'd almost forgotten him!'

While Miralles talked about his summers at Estrella de Mar and his friendship with Bolaño, I wondered how I would ask him for an interview; finally I resolved not to beat about the bush and to state the matter directly. Miralles didn't stop talking about Bolaño.

'So, what's become of him?'

'He's a writer,' I answered. 'He writes novels.'

'He wrote them back then, too. But no one wanted to publish them.'

'It's different now,' I said. 'He's a successful writer.'

'Really? I'm glad: I always thought he was talented, as well as an out-and-out liar. But I suppose you have to be an out-and-out liar to be a good novelist, don't you?' I heard a brief, dry, distant sound, like a laugh. 'Well, how can I help you?'

'I'm investigating an episode of the Civil War. The

execution by firing squad of some Nationalist prisoners at the Sanctuary of Santa María del Collell, near Banyoles. It was at the end of the war.' In vain I waited for Miralles' reaction. Impulsively I added: 'You were there, weren't you?'

During the interminable seconds that followed I could hear Miralles' gravelly breathing. Silently, exultantly, I realized I had struck home. When he began to speak again, Miralles' voice sounded darker and slower: completely different.

'Bolaño told you that?'

'I figured it out. Bolaño told me your story. He told me you spent the whole war with Líster, even retreating with him across Catalonia. Some of Líster's soldiers were at Collell just then, the same time as the execution. So you could easily have been one of them. You were, weren't you?'

Miralles was silent again; I heard his gravelly breathing again, and then a click: I thought he must have lit up a cigarette; a distant conversation in French fleetingly crossed the line. As the silence lengthened, I told myself I'd made a mistake, been too abrupt, but before I could try to rectify it, I finally heard:

'You said you were a writer, didn't you?'

'No,' I said. 'I'm a journalist.'

'Journalist.' Another silence. 'And you're planning to write about this? You really think any of your newspaper's readers are going to be interested in a story that happened sixty years ago?'

'I'm not going to write about it for the paper. I'm writing a book. Look, perhaps I've put it badly. I just want to talk to you for a while, so you can give me your version, so I can tell what really happened, or your version of what happened. It's

not a question of settling scores, it's about trying to understand —'

'Understand?' he interrupted me. 'Don't make me laugh!
You're the one who doesn't understand. A war is a war. And
that's all there is to understand. I know all too well, I spent
three years shooting off bullets for Spain, you know? And do
you think anyone's ever thanked me for it?'

'Precisely because of that —'

'Shut up and listen, young man,' he cut me off. 'Answer
me, do you think anyone's ever thanked me? I'll tell you the
answer: nobody. No one has ever thanked me for giving up
my youth, fighting for their fucking country. Nobody. Not a
single word. Not a gesture. Not a letter. Nothing. And now
you come along, sixty years later, with your shitty little
newspaper, or your book, or whatever, to ask me if I took part
in an execution by firing squad. Why don't you just accuse me
of murder straight out?'

'Of all the stories in History,' I thought as Miralles spoke,
'the saddest is Spain's, because it ends badly.' Then I thought:
'Does it end badly?' I thought: 'And damn the Transition!' I
said:

'I'm sorry you've misunderstood me, Señor Miralles —'

'Miralles, for Christ's sake, Miralles!' roared Miralles. 'No
one in my fucking life has ever called me Señor Miralles. My
name is Miralles, just Miralles. Got it?'

'Yes, Señor Miralles. I mean Miralles. But there is a
misunderstanding here. If you'll let me speak I'll explain.'
Miralles didn't say anything; I proceeded. 'A few weeks ago
Bolaño told me your story. I had just finished writing a book
about Rafael Sánchez Mazas. Have you heard of him?'

Miralles took his time answering, though clearly not because of any doubt.

'Of course. You're talking about the Falangist, aren't you? José Antonio's mate.'

'Exactly. He was one of the two people who escaped the firing squad at Collell. My book is about him, about the execution, about the people who helped him survive afterwards. And about one of Líster's soldiers who spared his life.'

'And what do I have to do with all of this?'

'The other fugitive from the firing squad left a testimony of the event, a book called *I Was Murdered by the Reds*.'

'What a title!'

'Yes, but the book's good, because it tells in detail what happened at Collell. What I don't have is any Republican version of what happened there, and without one my book's hamstrung. When Bolaño told me your story I thought perhaps you were at Collell too at the time of the execution and could give me your version of events. That's all I want: to chat with you for a while and for you to tell me your version. Nothing more. I promise I won't publish a single line without consulting you beforehand.'

Once again I heard Miralles' breathing, mixed in with the confused conversation in French that crossed the line again. When Miralles began to speak again his voice was as it had been at the beginning of our conversation, and I realized my explanation had managed to placate him.

'How did you get my phone number?'

I told him. Miralles laughed out loud.

'Look, Cercas,' he then began. 'Or do I have to call you Señor Cercas?'

172

'Call me Javier.'

'Okay, Javier. Do you know how old I am? Eighty-two. I'm an old man and I'm tired. I had a wife and I don't have her any more. I had a daughter and I don't have her any more. I'm still recovering from an embolism. I haven't got much time left, and the only thing I want is to be left alone. Listen, those stories don't interest anyone any more, not even those of us who lived through them; there was a time when they did, but not any more. Someone decided they had to be forgotten and, you know what I say? They were probably right. Besides, half of them are unintentional lies and the rest intentional ones. You're young; believe me I'm grateful for your call, but it would be best if you listened to me, if you forgot about this nonsense and devoted your time to something else.'

I tried to insist, but it was futile. Before hanging up, Miralles asked me to give his regards to Bolaño. 'Tell him I'll see him in Stockton,' he said. 'Where?' I asked. 'In Stockton,' he repeated. 'Tell him: he'll understand.'

Conchi exploded with joy when I phoned to tell her we'd found Miralles; then she exploded with rage when I told her I wasn't going to see him.

'After all this?' she screeched.

'He doesn't want to, Conchi. You have to understand.'

'And what's it matter to you that he doesn't want to?'

We argued. She tried to convince me. I tried to convince her.

'Look, do me a favour,' she finally said. 'Phone Bolaño. You never listen to me but he'll convince you. If you don't call him, I will.'

Partly because I was already planning to, and partly to

prevent Conchi from calling him, I phoned Bolaño. I told him about the conversation I'd had with Miralles and the old man's blank refusal of my proposal to go and see him. Bolaño said nothing. Then I remembered the message Miralles had given me for him; I told him.

'Damn the old guy,' muttered Bolaño, his voice self-absorbed and sardonic. 'He still remembers.'

'What's it mean?'

'The Stockton thing?'

'What else?'

After a long pause Bolaño answered my question with another question:

'Have you seen *Fat City*?' I said I had. 'Miralles really liked movies.' Bolaño went on. 'He'd watch them on the TV he had set up under the awning of his trailer; sometimes he'd go into Castelldefells and in one afternoon he'd watch three movies in a row, everything that was playing, he didn't care what was on. I usually took advantage of my few days off to go to Barcelona, but one time I ran into him on the seafront in Castelldefells, we went to have an *horchata* together and then he suggested I come to the pictures with him; since I didn't have anything better to do, I went with him. It might seem incredible that in a holiday resort town they'd be showing a John Huston film, but these things happened back then. Do you know what *Fat City* means? Something like "city of opportunities", or "fantastic city" or, even better, "some city!" Well, *some* sarcasm! Because Stockton, the city in the movie, is an atrocious city, where there aren't any opportunities for anybody – no opportunities except for failure, that is. For the most absolute and total failure, really. It's strange:

almost all boxing movies are about the rise and fall of the protagonist, about how they attain success and then they fail and are forgotten; not here. In *Fat City* neither of the protagonists – an old boxer and a young boxer – even glimpse the possibility of success, nor do any of those around them; like that old washed-up Mexican boxer, I don't know if you remember the one, he pisses blood before going into the ring, and enters and leaves the stadium alone, almost in darkness. Anyway, so that night, after the movie, we went to a bar, and ordered beer sitting at the bar and we were there talking and drinking until very late, facing a big mirror which reflected us and the bar, just like the two Stockton boxers at the end of *Fat City*; I think it was probably both the coincidence and the beer that made Miralles say at some point that we were going to end up the same, defeated and alone and punch-drunk in a dead-end city, pissing blood before going into the ring to fight to the death against our own shadows in an empty stadium. Miralles didn't say that, obviously, the words are mine, but he said something very similar. That night we laughed a lot and when we got back to the campsite it was practically daybreak, everyone was sleeping and the bar was closed, and we kept talking and laughing in that loose way that people laugh at funerals – or places like that, you know – and when we had said goodnight and I was going to my tent, stumbling along in the dark, Miralles called me and I turned and saw him: fat and lit by the pale light from a lamp-post, standing straight with his fist raised, and before his repressed laughter burst out again, I heard him whisper in the slumbering darkness of the campsite: "Bolaño, see you in Stockton!" And from that day on, every

175

time we said goodbye, whether it was until the next day or the next summer, Miralles always added: "See you in Stockton!"

We were left in silence. I suppose Bolaño was waiting for some sort of comment from me; I couldn't say anything, because I was crying.

'Anyway,' said Bolaño. 'What do you think you'll do now?'

'Fan-fucking-tastic!' shouted Conchi when I told her the news. 'I knew Bolaño would convince you! When do we leave?'

'We're not both going,' I said, thinking Conchi's presence might make the interview with Miralles easier to get. 'I'm going on my own.'

'Don't be silly! Tomorrow morning we'll get in the car and we'll be in Dijon in a jiffy.'

'I've already made up my mind,' I insisted emphatically, thinking that a trip to Dijon in Conchi's Volkswagen was riskier than Leclerc's column's march from the Maghreb to Chad. 'I'm going by train.'

So on Saturday evening I said goodbye to Conchi at the station ('Give Señor Miralles my regards', she said. 'He's called Miralles, Conchi,' I corrected her. 'Just Miralles'), and boarded a train to Dijon like someone boarding a train to Stockton. It was a sleeper, a night train, and I remember being in the restaurant car, with its springy leather seats and windows licked by the speed of the night, until very late, drinking and smoking and thinking about Miralles; at five in the morning, dishevelled, thirsty and sleepy, I stepped down into Dijon's underground and after walking along the deserted platforms illuminated by globes of weak light, I took a

176

taxi that dropped me off at the Victor Hugo, a little family-run hotel on the rue des Fleurs, not far from the city centre. I went up to my room, took a long drink of water from the tap, had a shower and lay down on the bed. In vain I tried to sleep. I thought about Miralles, whom I'd soon see, and about Sánchez Mazas, whom I'd never see; I thought about their one hypothetical encounter, sixty years earlier, almost a thousand kilometres from there, in the rain one violent morning in the forest; I thought I'd soon know if Miralles were the soldier of Líster's who spared Sánchez Mazas, and also what he'd thought as he looked him in the eye, and why he spared him, and that then perhaps I'd finally understand an essential secret. I thought all this and, while I thought, I started to hear the first sounds of the morning (footsteps in the hallway, the trill of a bird, a car's revving motor) and sense the dawn pushing against the window's shutters.

I got up, opened the window and the shutters: the uncertain light of the morning sun shone on a garden with orange trees and a quiet street lined by houses with sloping tiled roofs; only the birds' chirping broke the village-like silence. I got dressed and had breakfast in the hotel dining room; then, since I thought it was too early to go to the Nimphéas Residential Home, I decided to go for a walk. I'd never been to Dijon before, and not four hours earlier, as the taxi had crossed the streets which were lined with buildings like corpses of prehistoric animals, I had looked sleepily at its stately façades and bright blinking advertisements, and it had struck me as one of those imposing medieval cities that become ghostly at night and only then show their true face, the rotted skeleton of their former might; now, on the other hand, as soon as I got out onto the rue des Fleurs and, turning down rue des Roses and rue Desvoges, arrived at Place D'Arcy – which at that hour teemed with cars circling the Arc de Triomphe – it struck me as one of those sad provincial French cities where Simenon's sad husbands commit their sad crimes, a cheerless city with no future, just like Stockton. Although it was cool and the sun barely shone, I sat on the terrace of a bar, in Place Grangier, and had a Coca-Cola. To the right of the terrace, in a cobbled street, a little market was set up on the pavement, beyond which rose Notre Dame church. I paid for my Coke, and wandered through the market stalls looking at this and that, crossed the street and went into the church. At first I thought it was empty, but as I heard my footsteps echoing from the domed Gothic ceiling, I caught sight of a woman who'd just lit a candle at one of the side altars; now she was writing something in a bound notebook that was lying open on a lectern. When I approached the altar she stopped writing and turned to leave; our paths crossed in the middle of the nave, and I saw she was tall, young, pale, distinguished. Arriving at the altar, I couldn't help reading the last sentence written in the notebook: 'Please God, help me and my family in this time of darkness.'

I left the church, stopped a taxi and gave him the address of the Nimphéas Residential Home in Fontaine-Lès-Dijon. Twenty minutes later, we stopped on the corner of route des Daix and rue des Combottes, in front of a rectangular building with a pale green façade, which bristled with tiny balconies overlooking a garden with a pond and gravel paths. At the reception desk I asked for Miralles, and a girl with the unmistakable air and attire of a nun looked at me with a touch of curiosity or surprise and asked me if I were a relative. I told her I wasn't.

'A friend, then?'

'More or less,' I said.

'Room twenty-two,' and pointing down a corridor she added: 'but I saw him go that way a little while ago; he's probably in the television room, or in the garden.'

The corridor led into a big living room with enormous windows that opened onto a garden with a fountain and lawn chairs, where several old men were lying in the midday sun, tartan blankets covering their legs. In the living room were two old people – a woman and a man – sitting in imitation leather armchairs and watching TV; neither of them turned when I entered the room. I couldn't help but look at the man: a scar began at his temple, crossed his cheek, his jaw, went down his neck and disappeared under the fleece of his grey flannel shirt. I knew he was Miralles straightaway. Paralyzed, I hastily sought the words with which to approach him; but I didn't find them. As if sleepwalking, with my heart pounding in my throat, I sat down in the armchair next to his; Miralles did not turn, but an imperceptible movement of his shoulders revealed he'd noticed my presence. I decided to wait, I made myself comfortable in the chair, looked at the TV: on the screen the sun shone brilliantly, and a presenter with perfect hair and a hospitable air belied by the condescending rictus on his lips, gave instructions to the contestants.

'I expected you sooner,' murmured Miralles after a while, almost sighing, not taking his eyes off the screen. 'You're a bit late.'

I looked at his stony profile, his sparse grey hair, his beard growing like a minuscule forest of whitish bushes around the wild firebreak of the scar, the stubborn chin, the autumnal prominence of his belly tugging at the buttons of his shirt, and the strong hands speckled with spots, resting on a white cane.

'Late?'

'It's almost lunch time.'

I didn't say anything. I looked at the screen, now crammed with an array of domestic appliances; except for the pre-recorded and insistent voice of the presenter and the sounds of domestic chores coming from the corridor, the room was completely silent. Three or four armchairs away from Miralles, the woman was still sitting, motionless, with her cheek resting on a brittle hand, which was furrowed with blue veins; for a moment I thought she was asleep.

'Tell me, Javier,' Miralles spoke, as if we'd been talking for a long while and had stopped for a rest, 'do you like TV?'

'Yes,' I answered, and, transfixed by the cluster of whitish hairs sticking out of his nostrils, answered, 'But I don't watch it much.'

'I don't like it at all. But I watch it a lot: game shows, reports, films, spectaculars, news, everything. You know? I've lived here for five years, and it's like being shut out of the world. The newspapers bore me and I stopped listening to the radio a long time ago, so it's thanks to TV that I find out what's going on out there. This programme, for example,' scarcely lifting the tip of his stick to point at the television. 'I've never seen anything so stupid in my life: the people have to guess how much each of these things cost, and if they get it right, they keep it. But look how happy they are, look how they laugh.' Miralles went quiet, undoubtedly for me to appreciate for myself the pertinence of his observation. 'People today are much happier than they were in my day, anyone who's lived long enough knows that. That's why, every time I hear some old man fuming about the future, I know he's doing it to console himself because he's not going to be able to live through it, and every time I hear one of those intellectuals fume against TV I know I'm dealing with a cretin.'

Sitting up a little he turned his big, age-shrunken gladiator's body towards me and examined me with a pair of green eyes, which were strangely unmatched: the right, inexpressive and half-closed by the scar; the left wide open and inquisitive, almost ironic. I then realized that my initial impression of Miralles' face as petrified was only true for the side devastated by the scar; the other was vital, vehemently so. For a moment I thought it was like two people living together in the same body. Slightly intimidated by how close he was, I wondered whether the veterans of Salamis would also have had this derelict look of run-over old truck drivers.

'Do you smoke?' Miralles asked

I went to get my cigarettes out of my jacket pocket, but Miralles didn't let me finish.

'Not here.' Leaning on the arms of the chair and the walking stick, and unceremoniously rejecting my help ('Let go, let go, I'll ask you to lend me a hand when I need it'), he stood up laboriously and ordered: 'Come on, we're going for a walk.'

We were about to go out into the garden when a nun appeared from the corridor; she was about forty, dark-haired, smiling, tall and thin, wearing a white blouse and grey skirt.

'Sister Dominique told me you had a visitor, Miralles,' she said, holding out a pale, big-boned hand to me. 'I'm Sister Françoise.'

I shook her hand. Visibly uncomfortable, as if caught red-handed, holding the door half open Miralles introduced us: he said to me that Sister Françoise was the director of the home; he told her my name.

'He works for a newspaper,' he added. 'He's come to interview me.'

'Really?' The nun widened her smile. 'What about?'

'Nothing important,' said Miralles, beckonong me out into the garden with his expression. I obeyed. 'A murder. One that happened sixty years ago.'

'Oh good,' Sister Françoise laughed. 'It's about time you started confessing your crimes.'

'Go to hell, Sister,' Miralles said in farewell. 'You see,' he grumbled later on, as we walked beside a pond carpeted with water lilies and past a group of old men lying in hammocks, 'a whole lifetime spent railing against priests and nuns and here I am, surrounded by nuns who won't even let me smoke. Are you a believer?'

Now we were going down a gravel path bordered by boxwood hedges. I thought about the pale, distinguished-looking woman I'd seen that morning in the church of Notre Dame, lighting a candle and writing a supplication, but before I had time to answer the question, he answered it himself:

'What nonsense! There's nobody who believes any more, except for nuns. I'm not a believer either, you know. I lack imagination. When I die, what I'd like is for someone to dance on my grave, it'd be more cheerful, don't you think? Of course, Sister Françoise wouldn't be too pleased, so I suppose they'll say a mass and that'll be that. But that doesn't bother me, either. Did you like Sister Françoise?'

Since I didn't know whether or not Miralles liked her, I answered that I hadn't yet formed an opinion of her.

'I didn't ask you for your opinion,' answered Miralles. 'I asked if you liked her or not. If you can keep a secret, I'll tell you the truth: I like her a lot. She's good-looking, smart and nice. And young. What else can you ask for in a woman? If she wasn't a nun I'd have pinched her bum years ago. But, being a nun . . . to hell with it!'

We passed the front of the entrance to an underground parking lot, left the path and clambered down a small embankment – Miralles with surprising agility, clinging to his stick; me behind him, fearing he would fall at any moment – on the other side of which stretched a patch of lawn with a wooden bench overlooking the intermittent traffic of the rue des Combottes and facing a row of semi-detached houses lined up on the other side. We sat down on the bench.

'Okay,' said Miralles, leaning his stick on the edge of the bench, 'let's have that cigarette.'

I gave it to him, I lit it for him, then I lit one for myself. Miralles smoked with obvious enjoyment, inhaling the smoke deeply.

'Is smoking forbidden in the home?' I asked.

'Nah, it's just that hardly anybody smokes. The doctor made me give it up when I had the embolism. As if one thing had anything to do with the other. But sometimes I sneak into the kitchen, nick a cigarette off the cook and smoke it in my room, or out here. How do you like the view?'

I didn't want to subject him to an interrogation right away, and besides, I felt like listening to him talk about things, so we chatted away about his life in the home, Estrella de Mar, Bolaño. I could see that his mind was sharp and his memory intact and, as I vaguely listened to him, it occurred to me that Miralles was the same age my father would have been if he were still alive; this struck me as strange, stranger still that I'd thought of my father precisely at that moment and in that place. In a sense, I thought, although it had been more than six years since he'd died, my father still wasn't dead, because there was still someone remembering him. Or maybe it wasn't me remembering my father, but he who clung to my memory, so as not to die completely.

'But you haven't come here to talk about these things,' Miralles interrupted himself, at some point, a while after we'd thrown away our cigarette butts. 'You've come to talk about Collell.'

I didn't know where to start, so I just said:

'Then it's true you were at Collell?'

'Of course I was at Collell. Don't play the fool; if I hadn't been there, you wouldn't be here. Of course I was there – a week, maybe two, no more. It was at the end of January '39, I remember because the 31st of that month I crossed the border, I'll never forget that date. What I don't know is why we were there for so long. We were the remains of the V Corps of the Army of the Ebro, the majority of us veterans of the whole war, and we'd been firing away without a break since the summer until the front disintegrated and we had to make for the border like bats out of hell, with the Moors and the fascists hot on our heels. And all of a sudden, a few steps from France,

184

they made us stop. Sure, we were grateful, because we'd taken a hell of a beating; but we didn't understand what those days of truce were in aid of. There were rumours; there were some who said Líster was preparing the defence of Gerona, or a counterattack who knows where. Bullshit! We didn't have any weapons or ammunition or supplies or anything, really, we weren't even an army, just a bunch of wrecks who'd been hungry for months, scattered through the woods. But yeah, as I said, at least we got a rest. You know Collell?'

'A little.'

'It's not far from Gerona, near Banyoles. Some of them stayed there, others in the nearby villages; others were sent to Collell.'

'What for?'

'I don't know. Really, I don't think anyone knew. Don't you see? It was unimaginable pandemonium, every man for himself. Everybody gave orders, but nobody obeyed them. People deserted as soon as they got the chance.'

'And why didn't you desert?'

'Desert?' Miralles looked at me as if his brain weren't prepared to process the question. 'Well, I don't know. It didn't occur to me, I guess. At times like that it's not so easy to think, you know? Besides, where was I going to go? My parents had died and my brother was at the front too . . . Look,' he lifted his stick, as if something unexpected had come along to get him out of a fix, 'here they are.'

In front of us, on the other side of the grille that separated the garden of the residential home from the rue des Combottes, a group of small children were walking past, shepherded by two teachers. I regretted having interrupted

Miralles, because the question (or his inability to answer it; or perhaps it was just the children passing by) seemed to have disconnected him from his memories.

'You can set your watch by them,' he said. 'Have you got kids?'

'No.'

'Don't you like kids?'

'I like them,' I said, and thought of Conchi. 'But I don't have any.'

'I like them too,' he said, waving his stick at them. 'Look at that little rascal, the one in the hat.'

We sat in silence for a bit, watching the children. I didn't have to say anything, but philosophized inanely:

'They always seem so happy.'

'You haven't looked very closely,' Miralles corrected me. 'They never seem it. But they are. Just like us. What happens is that none of us notice, not us and not them.'

'What do you mean?'

Miralles smiled for the first time.

'We're alive, aren't we?' He stood up with the aid of his stick. 'Well then, it's time for lunch.'

As we walked back to the home I said:

'You were talking about Collell.'

'Would you mind giving me another cigarette?'

As if trying to bribe him, I gave him the whole pack. Putting it into his pocket he asked:

'What was I saying?'

'That it was pandemonium while you were there.'

'Sure.' He picked up the thread easily. 'Imagine the scene. There we were, what was left of the battalion; a Basque captain was in charge, a fairly decent guy, I can't remember his name right now, the commander had been killed in a bombing raid on the way out of Barcelona. But there were civilians there too, Carabineros, SIM agents. All kinds. I don't think anyone knew what we were doing there; waiting for the order to cross the border, I suppose, which was the only thing we could do.'

'Weren't you guarding the prisoners?'

He grinned sceptically.

'More or less.'

'More or less?'

'Yeah, of course we guarded them,' he gave in reluctantly. 'What I mean is that the ones in charge of the prisoners were the Carabineros. But, sometimes, when the prisoners went out for a walk or something, they ordered us to stay with them. If you call that guarding, I guess we guarded them.'

'And did you know who they were?'

'We knew they were big shots. Bishops, officers, fifth-column Falangists. People like that.'

We'd walked back up the gravel path; the old folks who minutes before had been sunning themselves had deserted their hammocks and were now chatting in groups at the entrance to the building and in the lounge where the television was still on.

'It's still early: let them go in,' said Miralles, taking me by the arm and forcing me to sit down beside him, at the edge of the pond. 'You wanted to talk about Sánchez Mazas, didn't you?' I nodded. 'They used to say he was a good writer. What do you think?'

'That he was a good minor writer.'

'And what does that mean?'

'That he was a good writer, but not a great writer.'

'So a person can be a good writer at the same time as being a huge son of a bitch. What a world!'

'Did you know Sánchez Mazas was at Collell?'

'Of course! How could I not know? He was the biggest of the big shots! We all knew. We had all heard of Sánchez Mazas and knew enough about him — I mean that thanks to him and four or five others like him what happened had happened. I'm not sure, but I think when he arrived at Collell, we'd already been there a few days.'

'Could be. Sánchez Mazas only arrived five days before they shot them. You told me before that you crossed the border on the 31st of January. The execution was the 30th.'

I was about to ask him if he'd still been at Collell that day, and if he remembered what happened, when Miralles, who'd started picking the earth out of the cracks between the paving stones with the tip of his stick, began to speak.

'The night before they'd told us to get our things together, because we'd be leaving the next day,' he explained. 'In the morning we saw a bunch of prisoners leave the Sanctuary escorted by some Carabineros.'

'Did you know they were going to shoot them?'

'No. We thought they were going to make them do some work or maybe swap them, there'd been a lot of talk of that. Although from the expressions on their faces it didn't really look like they were going to exchange them.'

'Did you know Sánchez Mazas? Did you recognize him among the prisoners?'

'No, I don't know . . . I don't think so.'

188

'You didn't know him or you didn't see him?'

'I didn't see him. Of course I knew him. How could I not have known him? We all knew him!'

Miralles swore that someone like Sánchez Mazas couldn't have gone unnoticed in a place like that, so just like all the rest of his comrades, he'd seen him many times, when he went out to walk in the garden with the other prisoners; he still vaguely remembered his thick glasses, his prominent nose, the sheepskin jacket in which, a few days later, he'd triumphantly relate his incredible adventure for Franco's cameras . . . Miralles fell quiet, as if the effort of remembering had left him momentarily exhausted. A faint sound of cutlery came from inside the building; in a fleeting glance I saw the television had been turned off. Miralles and I were alone in the garden now.

'And then?'

Miralles stopped digging with his stick and inhaled the clear midday air.

'Then nothing.' He exhaled slowly. 'The truth is I can't really remember, it was all so confused. I remember we heard shots and started running. Then someone shouted that the prisoners were trying to escape, so we started searching the woods to find them. I don't know how long the chase lasted, but once in a while you'd hear a shot, and they'd caught one of them. Anyway, I wouldn't be surprised if more than one escaped.'

'Two escaped.'

'Like I said, it doesn't surprise me. It had started to rain and the forest was pretty dense. Or at least that's how I remember it. Anyway, when we got tired of looking (or when someone gave the order) we went back to the Sanctuary, got the rest of our things together and that same morning we left.'

'In other words, according to you, there was no firing squad.'

'Don't put words in my mouth, young man. I'm just telling you how things were, or at least how I experienced them. The interpretation is your job, that's why you're a journalist, isn't it? Besides, you have to admit, if anybody deserved to be shot back then, Sánchez Mazas did; if they'd gotten rid of him in time, we might have been spared the war, don't you think?'

'I don't think anyone deserves to be shot.'

Miralles turned unhurriedly and looked at me steadily with his unmatched eyes, as if looking in mine for an answer to his ironic bewilderment; then an affectionate smile, that for a moment I feared would lead to a roar of laughter, softened the sudden toughness of his features.

'Don't tell me you're a pacifist!' he said, and put a hand on my collar bone. 'You might have told me that from the start! And while we're at it,' leaning on me, he stood up and pointed with his stick towards the home, 'let's see how you manage with Sister Françoise.'

I ignored Miralles' taunt and because I thought my time was running out, hastily asked:

'I'd like to ask you one last question.'

'Just one?' He spoke up to address the nun: 'Sister, the journalist wants to ask me one last question.'

'That's fine with me,' said Sister Françoise. 'But if the answer goes on too long, you're going to miss your lunch, Miralles.' Smiling at me, she added: 'Why don't you come back this afternoon?'

190

'Yes, young man,' Miralles agreed jovially. 'Come back this afternoon and we'll go on talking.'

We decided I'd come back about five, after his siesta and rehabilitation exercises. Along with Sister Françoise I accompanied Miralles to the dining room. 'Don't forget the tobacco,' Miralles whispered in my ear, in farewell. Then he went into the dining room, and as he sat down at a table between two white-haired old ladies who'd already started to eat, ostentatiously shot me a conspiratorial wink.

'What did you give him?' asked Sister Françoise as we walked towards the exit.

Since I thought she was referring to the pack of forbidden cigarettes that bulged in Miralles' shirt pocket, I blushed.

'Give him?'

'He seems very happy.'

'Ah,' I smiled with relief. 'We were talking about the war.'

'What war?'

'The war in Spain.'

'I didn't know Miralles had fought in that war.'

I was about to tell her that Miralles hadn't fought in one war, but many, but I couldn't, because I suddenly saw Miralles walking across the Libyan desert towards the Murzuk oasis – young, ragged, dusty and anonymous, carrying the tricolour flag of a country not his own, of a country that is all countries and also the country of liberty and which only exists because he and four Moors and a black guy are raising that flag as they keep walking onwards, onwards, ever onwards.

'Does anyone come to see him?' I asked Sister Françoise.

'No. At first his son-in-law used to come, his daughter's widower. But then he stopped coming; I think they fell out.

Miralles can be a slightly prickly character after all – I can tell you one thing though: he has a heart of gold.'

Listening to her talk about the embolism that paralysed Miralles' whole left side a few months ago, I thought how Sister Françoise spoke like the director of an orphanage trying to place an unruly pupil with a potential client; I also thought how Miralles was perhaps not an unruly pupil, but he certainly was an orphan, and then I wondered whose memory he'd cling to when he was dead so as not to die completely.

'We thought that was the end,' Sister Françoise went on. 'But he's recovered very well; he's got the constitution of an ox. He hasn't taken well to giving up smoking or eating without salt, but he'll get used to it.' When we got to the desk, she smiled and held out her hand. 'Well then, we'll see you this afternoon, won't we?'

Before leaving the residential home I looked at my watch: it had just gone twelve. I had five empty hours before me. I walked awhile along the route des Daix looking for a bar with a terrace where I could get something to drink, but, since I didn't find one anywhere – the neighbourhood was a network of wide suburban avenues with little semi-detached houses – as soon as I saw a taxi I stopped it and asked him to take me to the city centre. He dropped me off in a semi-circular plaza that opened onto the Palace of the Dukes of Burgundy. In front of its façade, sitting at a table on a terrace, I drank two glasses of beer. From where I was sitting I could see a sign with the name of the plaza: Place de la Libération. Inevitably I thought of Miralles entering Paris through the Porte-de-Gentilly the night of 24 August 1944, with the first Allied troops, on board his tank which would have been called Guadalajara or

192

Zaragoza or Belchite. Beside me, on the terrace, a very young couple were marvelling at the laughter and expressions of their pink baby, while busy, indifferent people walked by. I thought: Not a single one of these people knows of the existence of that practically one-eyed, dying old man who smokes cigarettes on the sly and at this very minute is eating without salt a few kilometres from here, but there's not a single one of them who's not indebted to him. I thought: No one will remember him when he's dead. I saw Miralles again, walking with the flag of the Free French across the infinite, burning sands of Libya, walking towards the Murzuk oasis while people were walking across this French plaza and across all the plazas in Europe going about their business, not knowing that their fate and the fate of the civilization they'd abdicated responsibility for depended on Miralles continuing to walk onwards, ever onwards. Then I remembered Sánchez Mazas and José Antonio and it occurred to me that perhaps they weren't so wrong and that at the eleventh hour it always has been a squad of soldiers that has saved civilization. I thought: What José Antonio and Sánchez Mazas could never imagine was that neither they nor anyone like them could ever form part of that eleventh-hour squad; on the contrary it would be formed by four Moors, a black guy, and a Catalan lathe operator who happened to be there by chance or bad luck, and who would have died laughing if anyone had told him he was saving us all in that time of darkness, and perhaps precisely for that reason – because he didn't imagine civilization at that moment depended on him – he was saving it and saving us, not knowing his final reward would be an unknown room in a residential home for the poor, in a sad city of a country that wasn't even his country, and where no one except maybe a smiling skinny nun, who didn't know he'd fought in the war, would miss him.

I ate lunch in the Café Central, in Place Grangier, very near to where I'd had breakfast that morning and, after drinking a coffee and a whisky at a café on rue de la Poste and buying a carton of cigarettes, returned to the Résidence des Nimphéas. It wasn't yet five when Miralles invited me up to his room and I noticed, not without surprise, that it wasn't the sordid institutional room I'd expected, but a neat, orderly and bright little apartment: one glance showed me a kitchen, a washroom, a bedroom and a little lounge with almost bare walls, two big armchairs, a table and big window onto a balcony open to the afternoon sun. I handed Miralles the carton of cigarettes in greeting.

'Don't be an idiot,' he said, tearing off the cellophane wrapper and taking out two packets. 'Where do you expect me to hide this?' He gave me back the rest of the carton. 'Would you like a nescafé? Decaffeinated, of course. They've forbidden me the real stuff.'

I didn't feel like one, but I accepted. As he made the coffee, Miralles asked me how I liked the apartment; I told him I liked it very much. He told me about the services (medical, recreational, cultural, cleaning) the home offered, and the rehabilitation exercises he had to do daily. When he'd finished making the coffee, I picked up the cups to take them into the lounge, but he motioned to me to stop; opening a low cupboard, he leaned half-way in with the agility of a contortionist and triumphantly brought out a hipflask.

'If you don't add a bit of this,' he remarked while pouring a shot in each cup, 'this stuff tastes like shit.'

Miralles put the flask back in its place, and then, each with our cup, we sat in the armchairs in the little lounge. I took a sip of nescafé; what Miralles had added was cognac.

'Now then,' said Miralles, amused, almost flattered, sitting back in his chair and stirring his nescafé. 'Shall we carry on with the interrogation? I assure you I've told you everything I know.'

I suddenly felt ashamed to keep asking him things, and felt like telling him that, even if I didn't have any questions to ask him, I'd be there anyway, chatting and drinking nescafé with him; for a moment I thought that I already knew everything I needed to know from Miralles, and, I don't know why, I remembered Bolaño and the night when he'd come across Miralles dancing a paso doble with Luz under the awning of his caravan and understood that his time at the campsite was up. In a flash I thought of Bolaño and my book, of *Soldiers of Salamis*, of Conchi and of the many months I'd spent searching for the man who'd saved Sánchez Mazas' life and for the meaning of a look and a shout in the woods, searching for a man who'd danced a paso doble in the garden of an improvised prison, sixty years earlier, just as Miralles and Luz had danced to another paso doble (or maybe the same one) in a working-class campsite in Castelldefells, under the awning of his improvised home. I didn't ask him anything, and said, as if it were a revelation:

'Sánchez Mazas survived the firing squad.' Miralles nodded, patiently, enjoying his nescafé with cognac. 'He survived thanks to a particular man,' I added. 'One of Líster's soldiers.'

I told him the story. When I'd finished, Miralles set his empty cup on the table and, leaning over a bit, and without getting out of the chair, he opened the balcony window and looked outside.

'Sounds like fiction, that story,' he said, in a neutral tone of voice, as he took a cigarette out of the half-empty pack from the morning.

I remembered Miquel Aguirre and said:

'Possibly. But all wars are full of stories that sound like fiction, aren't they?'

'Only for those who don't live through them.' He exhaled a plume of smoke and spat something out, perhaps a shred of tobacco. 'Only for those who tell them. For those who go to war to tell it, not to fight it. What was the name of that American novelist who entered Paris . . . ?'

'Hemingway.'

'Hemingway, that's it. What a clown!'

Miralles went quiet, distracted, as he watched the columns of smoke waving slowly in the still light on the balcony, through which the intermittent traffic noise reached us.

'And this story about Líster's soldier,' he started, turning back to me: the right half of his face had again taken on its stone-like appearance; on the left was an ambiguous expression of indifference and disappointment, almost annoyance. 'Who told you that?'

I explained. Miralles nodded, his mouth a circumflex, almost mocking. It was obvious the jovial spirit he'd welcomed me with that afternoon had disappeared. I didn't know what to say, but I knew I had to say something; but Miralles got in there first:

'Tell me something. You don't really care about Sánchez Mazas and his famous firing squad, right?'

'I don't know what you mean,' I said, quite honestly.

He looked into my eyes with curiosity.

'Got to hand it to you fucking writers!' he laughed. 'So what you were looking for was a hero. And I'm that hero, is that it? Can you believe it! But hadn't we decided you were a pacifist? Well, you know something? There aren't any heroes in peacetime, except maybe that little Indian guy who always went around half naked . . . And he wasn't even a hero, or only once they'd killed him. Heroes are only heroes when they die or get killed. The real heroes are born out of war and die in war. There are no living heroes, young man. They're all dead. Dead, dead, dead.' His voice cracked; after a pause, as he swallowed hard, he stubbed out his cigarette. 'Do you want another of these concoctions?'

He went to the kitchen with the empty cups. From the little lounge I heard him blow his nose; when he came back his eyes were shining, but he seemed to have calmed down. I suppose I must have tried to apologize for something, because I remember that, after handing me the nescafé and leaning back again in his armchair, Miralles interrupted me impatiently, almost irritated.

'Don't apologize, young man. You haven't done anything wrong. Besides, at your age you should know by now that a man doesn't apologize: he does what he does and says what he says, and then puts up with it. I'm going to tell you something you don't know, something about the war.' He took a sip of nescafé; so did I (Miralles had gone overboard with the cognac). 'When I left for the front in '36, these other boys went with me. They were from Terrassa, like me; very young – almost children – just like me; I knew some of them to see

197

them or to speak to, but most of them I didn't. There were the García Segués brothers (Joan and Lela), Miquel Cardos, Cagi Baldrich, Pipo Canal, el Gordo Odena, Santi Brugada and Jordi Gudayol. We fought the war together, both wars, ours and the other one, though they were both the same one. None of them survived. They all died. The last one was Lela García Segués. At first I got along better with his brother Joan, who was the same age as me, but in time Lela became my best friend, the best I've ever had: we were such good friends we didn't even have to talk when we were together. He died in the summer of '43, in a town near Tripoli, crushed by an English tank. You know what? Since the war ended, not a single day has gone by when I haven't thought about them. They were so young . . . They all died. All of them dead. Dead. Dead. All of them. None of them tasted the good things in life: none of them ever had a woman all to himself, none of them knew the wonder of having a child and of their child, at three or four years of age, climbing into his bed between him and his wife, on a Sunday morning, in a room full of sunshine . . .' At some point Miralles had started to cry: his face and his voice hadn't changed, but inconsolable tears streamed down the smooth channel of his scar, rolling more slowly down his unshaven cheeks. 'Sometimes I dream of them and then I feel guilty. I see them all: intact and greeting me with jokes, just as young as they were then, because time doesn't pass for them, they're just as young, and they ask me why I'm not with them – as if I'd betrayed them, because my true place was there; or as if I were taking the place of one of them; or as if in reality I had died sixty years ago in some ditch in Spain or Africa or France and I were dreaming a future life with a wife and children, a life that would end here, in this room in a home, chatting away to you.' Miralles kept talking, more quickly, without drying the tears that ran down his neck and soaked into his flannel shirt. 'Nobody remembers them, you know? Nobody. Nobody even remembers why they died, why they didn't have a wife and children and a sunny room; nobody remembers, least of all, those they fought for. There's no lousy street in any lousy town in any fucking country named after any of them, nor will there ever be. Understand? You understand, don't you? Oh, but I remember, I do remember, I remember them all, Lela and Joan and Gabi and Odena and Pipo and Brugada and Gudayol, I don't know why I do but I do, not a single day goes by that I don't think of them.'

Miralles stopped speaking, took out his handkerchief, dried his tears, blew his nose; he did it unabashed, as if it didn't embarrass him to cry in public, just like the ancient Homeric warriors, or a soldier of Salamis would have done. Then he gulped down the rest of his nescafé that had gone cold in the cup. We sat smoking in silence. The light on the balcony was fading; only an occasional car passed. I felt at ease, slightly inebriated, almost happy. I thought: He remembers for the same reason I remember my father and Ferlosio his and Miquel Aguirre his and Jaume Figueras his and Bolaño his Latin American friends, all of them soldiers killed in wars already lost: he remembers because, although they died sixty years ago, they're still not dead, precisely because he remembers them. Or perhaps it's not him remembering them, but them clinging to him, so they won't die off entirely. But when Miralles dies, I thought, his friends will die off, too, because there won't be anyone to remember them, to keep them from dying.

For a long time we chatted about other things, between nescafés, cigarettes and long silences, as if we hadn't just met that very morning. Then Miralles caught me sneaking a look at my watch.

'I'm boring you,' he interrupted himself.

'You're not boring me,' I answered. 'But my train leaves at eight-thirty.'

'Do you have to get going?'

'I think so.'

Miralles stood up from his armchair and picked up his stick. He said:

'I haven't been much help, have I? Do you think you'll be able to write your book?'

'I don't know,' I answered, truthfully; but then I said: 'I hope so.' And added: 'If I do, I promise I'll talk about your friends.'

As if he hadn't heard me, Miralles said:

'I'll see you out.' He pointed to the carton of cigarettes on the table. 'And don't forget those.'

We were about to leave the apartment when Miralles stopped.

'Tell me something.' He spoke with his hand on the doorknob; the door was half open. 'Why did you want to find the soldier who saved Sánchez Mazas?'

Without a moment's hesitation I answered:

'To ask him what he thought that morning, in the forest, after the execution, when he recognized Sánchez Mazas and looked him in the eye. To ask him what he saw in those eyes.

Why he spared him, why he didn't give him away, why he didn't kill him.'

'Why would he kill him?'

'Because in wars people kill people,' I said. 'Because thanks to Sánchez Mazas and four or five guys like him what happened had happened, and now that soldier was on his way to an exile with no way back. Because if anybody deserved to be shot it was Sánchez Mazas.'

Miralles recognized his words, nodded with a hint of a smile and, opening the door the rest of the way, gave me a tap on the back of the legs with his stick and said:

'Let's get going, we can't have you missing your train.'

We took the elevator down to the ground floor; from reception we called a taxi.

'Say goodbye to Sister Françoise for me,' I said, as we walked towards the exit.

'You're not planning to come back?'

'Not if you don't want me to.'

'Who said I didn't want you to?'

'In that case, I promise I'll come back.'

Outside, the light was rusty: it was dusk. We waited for the taxi at the garden gate in front of a traffic light that changed for nobody, because traffic at the intersection of route des Daix and rue Combotte was scant and the pavement deserted. On my right was an apartment building, not very high, with big picture windows and balconies overlooking the garden of the Nimphéas Residential Home. I thought it was a good place to live. I thought anywhere was a good place to live. I thought about Líster's soldier, and I heard myself say:

'What do you think he thought?'

'The soldier?' I turned to him. Leaning all his weight on his stick, Miralles watched the traffic light, which was red. When it changed from red to green, Miralles fixed me with a blank stare. 'Nothing,' he said

'Nothing?'

'Nothing.'

The taxi took a while. It was quarter to eight, and I still had to stop by the hotel to settle my bill and get my things.

'If you come back, bring me something.'

'Besides tobacco?'

'Yes.'

'Do you like music?'

'I used to. I don't listen to it any more; each time I do it makes me feel bad. I suddenly start thinking about what's happened to me, and especially what hasn't happened to me.'

'Bolaño told me you danced a pretty mean paso doble.'

'He said that?' he laughed. 'Fucking Chilean!'

'One night he saw you dancing to "Sighing for Spain" with a friend of yours, beside your caravan.'

'If you convince Sister Françoise, I can probably still dance it,' said Miralles, winking his scarred eye. 'It's a beautiful paso doble, don't you think? Look, here's your taxi.'

The taxi stopped at the corner, beside us.

'So,' said Miralles. 'I hope you come back soon.'

'I'll be back.'

'Can I ask you a favour?'

'Anything.'

Looking at the traffic light, he said:

'It's been a long time since I hugged anyone.'

I heard the sound of Miralles' stick falling to the ground, I felt his enormous arms squeezing me while mine could barely reach around him, I felt very small and very fragile, I smelled medicines and years of enclosure and boiled vegetables, and most of all old man, and knew that this was the unhappy smell of heroes.

We let go and Miralles picked up his stick and pushed me towards the taxi. I got in, gave the driver the address of the Victor Hugo, asked him to wait a moment and rolled down the window.

'There's one thing I didn't tell you,' I said to Miralles. 'Sánchez Mazas knew the soldier who spared him. One time he saw him dancing a paso doble in the gardens of Collell. Alone. The paso doble was "Sighing for Spain".' Miralles stepped off the kerb and came over to the taxi, leaning his big hand on the rolled-down window. I was sure I knew what the answer was going to be, because I didn't think Miralles could deny me the truth. Almost pleading, I asked him: 'It was you, wasn't it?'

After an instant's hesitation, Miralles smiled widely, affectionately, just showing his double row of worn-down teeth. His answer was:

'No.'

He took his hand off the window and ordered the taxi to start up. Then, abruptly, he said something that I didn't hear (maybe it was a name, but I'm not sure) because the taxi had started moving and though I stuck my head out the window and asked him what he'd said, it was already too late for him to hear me or answer me; I saw him raise his stick in a final farewell gesture and then, through the back window of the taxi, walk back to the home, slow, dispossessed, practically

203

one-eyed, and happy, with his grey shirt, his threadbare trousers and felt slippers, getting smaller and smaller against the pale green of the façade, his proud head, tough profile, his large, swaying and dilapidated body, supporting his unsteady steps with his stick, and when he opened the garden gate I felt a sort of premature nostalgia, as if, instead of seeing Miralles, I were already remembering him, perhaps because at that moment I thought I wasn't going to see him again, that I was always going to remember him like this.

I got my things from the hotel as fast as I could, paid the bill and arrived at the station just in time to catch the train. It was again a sleeper, very similar to the one I'd taken on the way here, maybe it was the same one. I settled into my compartment as I felt the train start off on its way. Then, down empty aisles carpeted in green, I made my way to the restaurant, a carriage with a double row of impeccably laid tables and springy seats of pumpkin-coloured leather. There was only one left. I sat down and, since I wasn't hungry, ordered a whisky. I savoured it, smoking, while on the other side of the window Dijon disintegrated in the twilight, soon converted into a series of crops barely visible in the growing darkness. Now the big window duplicated the restaurant car. It duplicated me: I looked fat and aged, a little sad. But I felt euphoric, immensely happy. I thought as soon as I got to Gerona, I'd phone Conchi and Bolaño and tell them what Miralles was like and about the city that was called Dijon, but whose real name was Stockton. I planned one, two, three trips to Stockton. I'd go to Stockton and take an apartment in the building on route des Daix, across from the residential home, and spend the mornings and afternoons chatting with Miralles, smoking cigarettes on the hidden bench or in his apartment, and later perhaps not chatting, not saying anything, just passing the time, because by then we'd be such good friends we wouldn't need to talk to enjoy being together; and at night I'd sit on the balcony of my apartment, with a pack of cigarettes and a bottle of wine and I'd wait until I saw that on the other side of the route des Daix the light in Miralles' apartment had been switched off, and then I'd stay there for a little while longer, in the dark, smoking and drinking while he slept or lay awake across the street, very near, lying in his bed and perhaps remembering his dead friends. And I regretted not having let Conchi come with me to Dijon and for a moment imagined the pleasure of being there with her and Miralles, and with Bolaño too, imagining that between the three of us we'd convince Bolaño to go to Dijon like someone going to Stockton, and Bolaño would go to Stockton with his wife and his son, and the six of us would hire a car and go on outings to the surrounding villages; we'd form an odd, impossible family and then Miralles would finally stop being an orphan (and perhaps so would I) and Conchi would feel a terrible longing to have a child (and perhaps so would I). I also imagined that one day, not too late in the evening, Sister Françoise would call me at my house in Gerona, I'd call Conchi at her house in Quart and then Bolaño at his house in Blanes; and the three of us would leave the next day for Dijon although where we'd arrive would be Stockton, finally Stockton – and we'd have to empty Miralles' apartment, throw out his clothes and sell or give away his furniture and keep a few things, very few because Miralles undoubtedly kept very few things, perhaps the odd photograph of him smiling happily between his wife and daughter or in a soldier's uniform among other young men in soldiers' uniforms, not much more, who knows, maybe an old vinyl record of scratchy old *paso-doble*s that no one had listened to for ages. And there would be a funeral and a burial, and at the burial music, the cheerful music of a sorrowful paso doble playing on a scratched vinyl record; and then I'd take Sister Françoise by the hand and ask her to dance with me beside Miralles' grave, I'd insist that she dance to a music she didn't know how to dance to on Miralles' fresh grave, in secret, so no one would see us – so no one in Dijon or in France or in Spain or in all of Europe would know that a good-looking, clever nun (with whom Miralles always wanted to dance a paso doble and whose bum he never dared touch) and a provincial journalist were dancing in an anonymous cemetery of a melancholy city beside the grave of an old Catalan Communist, no one would know except a nonbelieving and maternal fortune-teller and a Chilean lost in Europe who would be smoking, his eyes clouded, standing back a little and very serious, watching us dance a paso doble beside Miralles' grave just as one night years before he'd seen Miralles and Luz dance to another paso doble under the awning of a trailer in the Estrella de Mar campsite, seeing it and wondering if maybe that paso doble and this one were in fact the same, wondering without expecting an answer, because he already knew that the only answer is that there is no answer, the only answer is a sort of secret or unfathomable joy, something verging on cruelty, something that resists reason, but nor is it instinct: something that remains there with the same blind stubbornness with which blood persists in its course and the earth in its immovable orbit and all beings in their obstinate condition of being, something that eludes words the way the water in the stream eludes stone, because words are only made for saying to each other, for saying the sayable, when the sayable is everything except what rules us or makes us live or matters or what we are or what that nun is and that journalist who is me dancing beside Miralles' grave as if their lives depended on that absurd dance or like someone asking for help for themselves and their family in a time of darkness. And there, sitting in the soft pumpkin-coloured seat in the restaurant car, rocked by the clattering of the train and the whirlwind of words spinning round unceasingly in my head, with the bustle of passengers dining around me and my almost empty glass of whisky in front of me, and in the window, beside me, the distant image of a sad man who couldn't be me but was me, there I suddenly saw my book, the book I'd been after for years, I saw it there in its entirety, finished, from the first line to the last, there I knew that, although nowhere in any city of any fucking country would there ever be a street named after Miralles, if I told his story, Miralles would still be alive in some way and if I talked about them, his friends would still be alive too, the García Segués brothers – Joan and Lela – and Miquel Cardos and Gabi Baldrich and Pipo Canal and el Gordo Odena and Santi Brugada and Jordi Gudayol would still be alive even though for many years they'd been dead, dead, dead, dead, I'd talk about Miralles and about all of them, not leaving a single one out, and of course about the Figueras brothers and Angelats and Maria Ferré, and also about my father and even Bolaño's young Latin Americans, but above all about Sánchez Mazas and that squad of soldiers that at the eleventh hour has always saved civilization and in which he wasn't worthy to serve but Miralles was, about those inconceivable moments when all of civilization depends on a single man, and about that man and about how civilization repays that man. I saw my book, whole and real, my completed true tale, and knew that now I only had to write it, put it down on paper because it was in my head from start ('It was the summer of 1994, more than six years ago now, when I first heard about Rafael Sánchez Mazas facing the firing squad') to finish, an ending where an old journalist, unsuccessful and happy, smokes and drinks whisky in the restaurant car of a night train that travels across the French countryside among people who are having dinner and are happy and waiters in black bow-ties, while he thinks of a washed-up man who had courage and instinctive virtue and so never erred or didn't err in the one moment when it really mattered, he thinks of a man who was honest and brave and pure as pure and of the hypothetical book which will revive him when he's dead, and then the journalist watches his sad, aged reflection in the window licked by the night until slowly the reflection dissolves and in the window appears an endless and burning desert and a lone soldier, carrying the flag of a country not his own, of a country that is all countries and only exists because that soldier raises its abolished flag; young, ragged, dusty and anonymous, infinitely tiny in that blazing sea of infinite sand, walking onwards beneath the black sun of the window, not really knowing where he's going or who he's going with or why he's going, not really caring as long as it's onwards, onwards, onwards, ever onwards.

208

Notes

p.4 Rafael Sánchez Ferlosio (1927–): Considered one of the most notable Spanish writers of his generation. Two of his early novels have been translated into English: *Adventures of the Ingenious Alfanhui* (trans. Margaret Jull Costa, 2000) and his very influential 1956 novel, *El Jarama*, as *The River* (trans. Margaret Jull Costa, 2003).

p.6 Franco, Francisco (1892–1975): General of the Spanish Army. One of the conspirators in the military revolt against the Republican government in July 1936, after an initial hesitation he became the leader of the Nationalist forces during the course of the war. He ruled Spain from the end of the Civil War until his death.

p.6 José Antonio Primo de Rivera (1903–1936): Son of Miguel Primo de Rivera (dictator from 1923-1930), one of the founders of the Spanish Falange (see afterword), and its undisputed leader until his death in November 1936 made him the first martyr of Spanish fascism. He is generally referred to in Spain simply as José Antonio.

p.9 Antonio Machado (1875–1939): One of the greatest Spanish poets of the twentieth century. During the war he was a tireless supporter of the Republic in his writing and became a symbol of resistance to fascism.

p.10 Manuel Machado (1874–1947): Spanish poet and dramatist. Often referred to as 'the bad Machado' in contrast to his famous and revered brother Antonio, both for having failed to support the Republic and for the decline in quality of his literary output. The plays they wrote together influenced Lorca and his poetry was admired by Jorge Luis Borges among others.

p.17 nationalist: Supporter of regional (in this case, Catalan) autonomy or independence. [Translator's note: 'Nationalists' is in this context written with a lower-case 'n' to avoid confusion with Franco-supporting Nationalists (*Nacionales*).]

p.18 Generalitat: Regional autonomous government of Catalonia.

p.19 *checas*: Improvised prisons in the Republican zone where justice was imposed by 'popular, revolutionary' tribunals. *Checas*, as the Russian-derived name suggests, were especially prevalent in areas controlled by socialist or Communist parties or trade unions.

p.19 SIM: *Servicio de Información Militar*, or Military Information Service, the political police organization created by Indalecio Prieto (see note p.72) in August 1937 but almost immediately taken over by the Communists, was a rationalization of the various intelligence services within the Republican forces. Previously the Army, the foreign ministry, the Catalan regional government, the Basque regional government in exile, the Carabineros, the International Brigades, etc., had each run their own 'counter-espionage' networks.

p.19 Líster, Enrique (1907–1994): Moscow-trained colonel of Republican army. He commanded the Fifth Regiment, a legendary Communist unit that defended Madrid from the Nationalist onslaught in the early stages of the war. Later he fought in the Second World War as a general in the Soviet Army and organized guerrilla actions against the Franco regime in the late 1940s.

p.25 old shirts: Original members of the Spanish Falange and later members of FET (see note p.67) loyal to original 'revolutionary' ideals of the Falange as opposed to the ultra-Catholic, arch-conservative values of their imposed allies and the many people who joined the party as the Nationalists gained ground during the course of the war.

p.26 Ridruejo, Dionisio (1912–1975): Spanish poet. Leading member of the Falange before and during the war, later to become a democratic opponent of the Franco regime.

p.67 *Falange Española Tradicionalista y de la JONS*, usually called the FET, was an amalgamation of the Carlist (ultra-Catholic and monarchist, supporters of a rival claimant line to the throne, their principal party was called *Comunión Tradicionalista*) and fascist parties, forcibly united by Franco in April 1937 and thereafter the only legal party in Nationalist Spain.

p.72 Indalecio Prieto (1883–1962): Moderate socialist leader. Republican Minister of Air Force and Navy and later Minister of Defence.

p.89 Carabineros: The border police force in pre-war Spain, a majority of them stayed loyal to the Republic after the uprising, fighting with the militias and later as an elite force within the Popular Army.

A NOTE ON THE AUTHOR

Javier Cercas was born in 1962. He is a novelist, short-story writer and essayist, whose books include *El móvil* (The Motive, 1987, revised edition 2003), *El inquilino* (The Tenant, 1989), *El vientre de la ballera* (The Belly of the Whale, 1997) and *Relatos reales* (True Tales, 2000). In the 1980s he taught for two years at the University of Illinois, and since 1989 has been a lecturer in Spanish Literature at the University of Gerona. He is a regular contributor to the Catalan edition of *El País*. *Soldiers of Salamis* has been filmed by David Trueba for release in 2003 and is being published in fifteen languages.

Anne McLean has translated Latin-American and Spanish novels, short stories, memoirs and other writings by authors including Carmen Martín Gaite, Orlando González Esteva, Julio Cortázar, Paula Varsavsky, Ignacio Padilla and Luis Sepúlveda.

A NOTE ON THE TYPE

The text of this book is set in Fournier. Fournier is derived from the *romain du roi*, which was created towards the end of the seventeenth century for the exclusive use of the Imprimerie Royale from designs made by a committee of the Académie of Sciences. The original Fournier types were cut by the famous Paris founder Pierre Simon Fournier in about 1742. These types were some of the most influential designs of the eighteenth century, and are counted among the earliest examples of the 'transitional' style of typeface. This Monotype version dates from 1924. Fournier is a light, clear face whose distinctive features are capital letters that are quite tall and bold in relation to the lower-case letters, and *decorative italics, which show the influence of the calligraphy of Fournier's time.*